Praise for

The O'CONNELLS

by Sandra Marton

"This first book of the O'Connell series,
Keir O'Connell's Mistress, vibrates with charismatic
characters and a tight, page-turning plot. No one
delivers consistent must-reads like Sandra Marton!"
—*Romantic Times*

"Romance does not get better than a Sandra Marton
story. *The Sicilian Surrender* has power and passion
evident in the strength and compassion of an exquisite
hero and the heroine's courage to create a new life.
Together they are a formidable couple."
—*Romantic Times*

More praise for Sandra Marton

"When passion ignites in the tale
it is really hot enough to burn!"
—*A Romance Review* on *Marriage on the Edge*

"Powerful characterizations, intense emotions, sizzling
sensual chemistry and a flair for the unexpected...
Ms. Marton has a unique way of pulling readers
deep into the story right from the beginning."
—*The Best Reviews* on
Cole Cameron's Revenge

"*The Pregnant Mistress*...has sensational characters,
a superb storyline, sensual scenes and
an intense conflict."
—*Romantic Times*

Dear Reader,

Some images and ideas are impossible to resist. A while back, I read an article about a woman who'd risen to the highest ranks in the corporate world and how difficult it had been for her to get there. She talked about the men who'd insisted on seeing her solely as an unqualified female, and about the one man who'd never viewed her that way...the man she fell in love with and eventually married.

And I thought, what if that man had not been so open-minded? What if he, too, had seen her as nothing but trouble—but trouble in the best possible way? What if he were a sheikh, sexy and gorgeous and arrogant as hell? And what if fate brought them together, despite their initial dislike of each other, and forced them into a marriage neither wants?

Welcome to *The Sheikh's Convenient Bride,* and to a love affair hot enough to set the desert on fire.

With love,

Sandra

Sandra Marton

THE SHEIKH'S CONVENIENT BRIDE

The O'CONNELLS

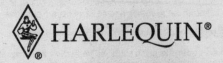

HARLEQUIN®

TORONTO • NEW YORK • LONDON
AMSTERDAM • PARIS • SYDNEY • HAMBURG
STOCKHOLM • ATHENS • TOKYO • MILAN • MADRID
PRAGUE • WARSAW • BUDAPEST • AUCKLAND

ISBN 0-373-12410-4

THE SHEIKH'S CONVENIENT BRIDE

First North American Publication 2004.

This edition published by arrangement with Harlequin Books S.A.

® and TM are trademarks of the publisher. Trademarks indicated with
® are registered in the United States Patent and Trademark Office, the
Canadian Trade Marks Office and in other countries.

www.eHarlequin.com

Printed in U.S.A.

CHAPTER ONE

HE WAS a sheikh, the King of Suliyam, a small nation sitting on an incredible deposit of oil on the tip of the Bezerian Peninsula.

On top of that, he was tall, dark-haired, gray-eyed and gorgeous.

If you liked the type.

According to the tabloids and the TV celebrity-tell-all shows, most women did.

But Megan O'Connell wasn't most women. Besides, tall, dark, handsome and disgustingly rich didn't begin to make up for egotistical, self-centered, and arrogant.

Megan raised her coffee cup to her lips. Okay. Maybe that was superfluous. So what? Men like him were superfluous, too. What did the world need with penny-ante dictators who thought they were God's gift to the female sex? To everybody on the planet, when you came down to it?

She'd never exchanged a word with the man but she didn't have to, to know what he was like. Her boss—another egotistical jerk, though not a good-looking one—had transmitted the sheikh's message to her this morning and it had been clear as glass.

She was a female. That made her a second-class citizen in his eyes. He, of course, was male. As if that weren't enough, he was royalty.

Royalty. Megan's lip curled with contempt. What he was, was a chauvinist pig. How come she was the only one who seemed to notice? She'd been watching him charm the little group at the other end of the boardroom for almost an hour, tilting his head when one of them spoke as if he really gave a damn what that person was saying.

If only they knew what an SOB like him could do to someone.

She had to admit, he seemed good at what he did. Holding the attention of a bunch of self-important partners and managers of a prestigious financial firm wasn't easy but then, if you believed the Times, he was the leader of his nation's cautious steps into modernity and development.

If you believed the Times. It seemed more logical to believe the tabloids. According to them, he was a playboy. A heartbreaker on three continents.

That, Megan thought, was undoubtedly closer to the truth.

The only thing she was sure of was that he was Qasim al Daud al Rashid, King of Suliyam since his father's death and the Absolute Ruler of his People.

It was a title that would have gone over big a couple of generations ago. Too bad the sheikh didn't seem to care that such nonsense was a joke now…though it didn't seem a joke to what passed for the news media, or here in the Los Angeles offices of Tremont, Burnside and Macomb, Financial Advisors and Consultants.

Too bad she'd accepted the transfer from Boston, where nobody would have made this kind of fuss over a walking, talking anachronism.

"Oh, your highness," a woman said, the words accompanied by a sigh that carried the length of the room.

His Highness, indeed. That was the proper way to address the king, according to the belly-crawling sycophants in his entourage. Megan drank the last of her coffee. No way would she ever call him that. If she had the misfortune to speak with the man—which she surely wouldn't, after what had happened this morning—she'd sooner choke. His High and Mightiness was more like it. What else would you call a twenty-first century dictator leading a 16th century life? Someone who'd single-handedly set her career back five years?

The bastard.

To think she'd worked her tail off, researching and writing the proposal that had won him as a client. To think she'd spent days and evenings and weekends on the thing. To think she'd dreamed about what handling such a prestigious account would mean to her career, swallowed all those little hints that she'd be named a partner, believed they were soon to become reality.

Every bit of it had gone up in a puff of smoke this morning, when Simpson told her he was giving the Suliyam assignment to Frank Fisher instead of her.

Megan started to refill her cup, thought better of it—she was already flying on caffeine—and poured herself a Mimosa instead. The vintage Krug and fresh OJ were there because the sheikh supposedly liked an occasional Mimosa at brunch, thanks to the influence, some said, of the genes of his California-born mother.

He'd never know it but he was drinking them today, assuming he was drinking them, thanks to Megan's research. She'd learned about the Mimosas and ordered the champagne and the orange juice.

If only she'd ordered strychnine instead.

Damn, she had to stop thinking this way. She had to stop thinking, period, or she'd say something, do something that would cost her her job.

As if she already hadn't.

No. Why think like a defeatist? She wouldn't lose her job. She'd put in too much time and effort at Tremont, Burnside and Macomb to let that happen. She would not let the decision made by The King of All He Surveyed ruin her career. There'd be other big accounts, other career-changing clients.

Of course there would.

If only her worm of a boss hadn't waited until today to break the news.

She'd come in early, eight o'clock, to make sure she was ready for the meeting with the sheikh. She'd even checked with the caterer to make sure he'd be coming on time, bringing little sandwiches and pastries, the brand of coffee the sheikh was known to favor, the champagne and the juice. Fresh juice, she'd reminded the caterer, and vintage champagne.

By 8:10, she knew everything was ready. The caterer. The boardroom. The manager of this Los Angeles branch of Tremont, Burnside and Macomb, Jerry Simpson.

Quarter past eight, Jerry had stepped into her office, a smile on his pudgy face and a Starbucks' container in his outstretched hand.

"For you," he'd said.

She almost said *Thanks, but I've been drinking coffee for two hours straight...* But why turn down the friendly gesture? Jerry never came in early. He never brought her coffee. Mostly he never smiled. He never sat down beside her desk, either, the way he did as she took the container from him.

With the benefit of hindsight, Megan realized that warning bells should have gone off right there and then. Fool that she was, she'd simply figured Jerry was there early so they could get ready for the important meeting together.

"How was your weekend?" Jerry said.

She'd spent it on Nantucket Island at her brother's wedding, so it was easy to smile and say "Great," because it had been. He smiled back, said that was good to hear and didn't she look wonderful and oh, by the way, he was giving the Suliyam account to Frank Fisher.

Megan blinked. She told herself she'd misunderstood. How could he give her client to somebody else? Maybe she'd had too much champagne at Cullen's wedding, too little sleep, too many cups of coffee to try to get her brain in gear after the alarm went off this morning.

Simpson couldn't have said what she'd thought he'd said, so she gave a little laugh.

"For a minute there, Jerry, I thought you said—"

"I did," Simpson replied, and she looked beyond his smarmy smile and saw that he was telling the truth.

"But that's impossible," she said slowly, while she tried to make sense of what was happening. "Suliyam commissioned a study—"

"The sheikh commissioned it."

"Whatever. The point is—"

"It's an important detail, Megan." Simpson smoothed his hand over the pinstripes straining across his tiny potbelly. "His Highness speaks for his country."

"I don't see what that—"

"To all intents and purposes, he *is* Suliyam."

"The point is," Megan said impatiently, "I did all the work on this report. I did it because you said the king would be my client, if he signed on—"

"I never told you that. I simply asked you to prepare the proposal."

Megan narrowed her eyes. "It's standard practice in this firm that the person who works up the data for a client gets that client."

"You are not a partner, Megan."

"A formality, Jerry. You know that."

"His Highness wants someone with authority."

"Well, that's easily resolved. Make me a partner now instead of waiting until July."

"Megan." Simpson got to his feet, an unconvincing smile of sympathy curving his thin lips. "I'm truly sorry this has happened, but—"

"It hasn't happened. Not yet. All the partners have to do is vote me in and tell the sheikh I'm more than capable of—"

"You're a woman."

That had stopped her. "Excuse me?"

Simpson gave a deep sigh. "It's nothing personal. It's not you per se. It's only that—"

"That what?" She was still trying to sound civil. Not an easy thing when your wimp of a boss told you the job you'd been counting on, an assignment so sweet it had every other accountant in the office panting for it, wasn't going to be yours after all. "Come on, Jerry. What has my being a woman to do with anything?"

"Actually," her boss said, smoothly avoiding the question, "it's for the best. I need you to handle a new client. Rod Barry, the big Hollywood director."

"The Sheikh of Suliyam is the client I want." Megan rose from her chair and put her hands on her hips. "He's the client you promised me."

"Barry's a tough cookie. It'll take special skills to work with him. You're the only one I can count on to do the job. Do the great work I know you'll do and you're up for a partnership next year." Simpson stuck out his hand. "Congratulations."

If Megan had been born yesterday, maybe she'd have fallen for the whole routine, but twenty-eight years of living, a dual degree in economics and accounting, a master's degree in finance and a hard-won slip of paper that said she was a Certified Public Accountant meant she was neither innocent, stupid, nor easily bought off.

And then there was that little remark about her being female.

Her boss was trying to bribe her into accepting her fate. Why? The truth was, he had the authority to take this job away from her. Why would he be trying to buy her off? There had to be a reason.

"Back up a little," Megan said slowly. "You said I was a woman and that was a problem."

"I didn't say that. Not exactly. All I meant was—"

"Why is it a problem?"

Simpson folded his lips in so they all but disappeared. "Suliyam is a kingdom."

"I'm fully aware of that. There's a description of Suliyam's structure in my proposal."

"It has no constitution, no elected representatives—"

"Damn it, Jerry, that's what a kingdom is! I spent three months doing the research."

"Then you also know that its people live by traditions that might seem a bit, ah, old-fashioned to us."

"Would you please get to the point?"

Simpson's attempts to avoid the issue vanished. "You don't want to handle the new account, then the best I can do is assign you to Frank Fisher as his assistant. He'll go to Suliyam, you'll stay here and execute the orders he sends."

"No way am I going to play second fiddle to Fisher!"

"This discussion is over, Megan. You're off the account. The sheikh wants it that way, and that's the way it will be."

"The sheikh," Megan said coldly, "is an idiot."

Simpson had turned a deathly shade of white. He shot a look at her office door as if he expected to see the sheikh standing there with a sword in his hand.

"You see?" he hissed. "Aside from anything else, there's one reason you're not suitable for this assignment."

Dumb, Megan told herself, dumb, dumb, dumb!

"You know I'd never say such a thing to him."

"You'd never get the chance." Simpson stuck out his jaw. "Or didn't you notice, when you did your research, that women don't have the same privileges there as they do here? They have no status in the sheikh's world. Not as we understand it, anyway."

"What women have here," Megan said coldly, "aren't privileges, they're rights. As for the sheikh…he spends as much time in the west as he does in his own country. He deals with women ambassadors at the United Nation. You can't actually mean—"

"Our representative will have to work at his side. Deal with his people. Do you think, for one minute, those men agree to sit down with a woman, much less take criticism and suggestions from her?"

"What I think is that it's time they joined the twenty-first century."

"Getting them to do that isn't the function of Tremont, Burnside and Macomb."

"I also think," Megan said in a dangerously soft voice, "that *you'd* better join this century, too. I'm sure you've heard of anti-discrimination laws."

Simpson proved ready for that threat. "Anti-discrimination laws are valid only within the United States. There are place where even our female soldiers conform to local customs."

"What the military does has nothing to do with the sheikh's plan to raise capital to further develop Suliyam's resources," Megan snapped, though a lurch in her belly told her she'd just lost ground.

"It has everything to do with it."

"I doubt if a judge would agree."

Simpson slapped his hands on her desk and leaned toward her. "If you're threatening to sue us, Miss O'Connell, go right ahead. Our attorneys will make mincemeat out of your case. The laws of Suliyam take precedence over American law when our employees live and work there."

Was he right? Megan wasn't sure. For all she knew, Simpson might have already trotted the issue past the company's legal counsel.

"And, knowing the outcome, if you were still foolish enough to go ahead with a lawsuit," Simpson added with smug self-assurance, "what would you put on your résumé? That you sued your employers rather than follow their wishes? How many jobs do you think that would get you?"

Zero, but Megan wasn't going to admit that. "That's blackmail!"

"It's the truth. You'd be poison to any firm of financial advisors."

Her stomach took another dip. He was right. Legally, you couldn't pay a penalty for bringing an anti-discrimination lawsuit. Practically, things weren't quite that simple.

Simpson smiled slyly. "Besides, we never really had this conversation. I only stopped by to thank you for the fine work you did on that proposal and to tell you, sadly enough, that you don't have quite the experience you'd need to take on the job yourself. I'm sure you'll gain a world of experience staying here in the States and being Fisher's diligent assistant." Her boss rocked up on his toes, which elevated him to at least five foot five. "Nothing wrong with any of that, Miss O'Connell. Nothing at all."

Megan stared at him. He was a worm, but he was right. She probably didn't have grounds for suing the company. Even if she did, doing so would end her career.

She was stuck. Cornered, with no valid options.

The logical thing was to choke back her rage, pin a smile to her lips and thank Simpson for telling her she was going to become a partner and that she'd be thrilled to take on an important new client in the film business.

But she couldn't. She couldn't. She'd always believed in playing by the rules and Jerry Simpson was telling her the rules didn't mean a thing. He was beaming at her now, certain he had her beat.

He didn't.

"You're wrong," she said quietly. "Wrong about me, Jerry. I'm not going to let you and the Prince of Darkness shove me aside."

Simpson's smile tilted. "Don't be stupid, Megan. I just told you, you can't win a suit against us."

"Maybe not, but think of the publicity! It'll be bad for you—we both know what the senior partners think about negative publicity. And it'll be worse for the sheikh. Suliyam's floating on a sea of oil and minerals, but once investors hear his backward little country's up to its neck in a human rights lawsuit, I'll bet they'll gallop in the other direction."

Simpson wasn't smiling at all now. Good, Megan thought, and leaned in for the kill.

"You yank this job away from me," she said, "I'll see to it that Suliyam's dirty linen is hung out for the world to see." She stepped past her boss, then turned and faced him one last time. "Be sure and tell the exalted Pooh-Bah that, Mr. Simpson."

It had seemed the perfect exit line and she'd stalked away, realizing too late that she'd abandoned her own office, not Simpson's, but no way in hell would she have turned back.

As for her threat—she wouldn't take that back, either, even though it was meaningless. She knew it and she didn't doubt that Simpson knew it, too. He was an oily little worm but he wasn't stupid.

Her career meant everything to her. She'd devoted herself to it. She wasn't like her mother, who'd cheerfully handed her life over to a man so he could do with it as he chose. She wasn't like her sister, Fallon, whose beauty had been her ticket to independence. She wasn't like her sister, Bree, who seemed content to drift through life.

No, Megan had thought as she yanked open the ladies' room door, no, she'd taken a different path. Two degrees. Hard work. A steady climb to the top in a field as removed from the glittery world of chance in which she'd grown up as night was from day.

Was she really going to toss it all aside to make a feminist point?

She wasn't.

She wasn't going to sue anyone, or complain to anyone, or do much of anything except, when she got past her fury, swallow her pride and tell Jerry she'd thought things over and—and—

God, apologizing would hurt! But she'd do it. She'd do it. Nobody had ever said life was easy.

So Megan had stayed in the ladies' room until she figured the coast was clear. Then she'd started for her office, brewed a pot of coffee, dug out her secret stash of Godiva and spent the next hour mainlining caffeine while she thought up imaginative ways to rid the world of men.

A little before ten, the PA she shared with three other analysts popped her head in.

"He's here," she'd whispered.

No need to ask who. Only one visitor was expected this morning. Plus, Sally had that look teenage girls got in the presence of rock stars.

"I'm happy for you," Megan replied.

"Mr. Simpson says...he says he would like you to stay where you are."

"I would like Mr. Simpson in the path of a speeding train," Megan said pleasantly, "but we do not always get what we want."

"Megan," Sally said with urgency, "you're wired. All that coffee...and, oh wow, you put away half that box of chocolate. You know what happens when you have too much caffeine!"

She knew. She got edgy. She got irritable. She talked too much. A good thing she realized all that, or she'd show up in the boardroom despite what Simpson would like. Hell, she'd show up *because* of what he'd like.

Yes, it was a good thing she knew Sally was right. Staying put was a good idea.

"Tell Mr. Simpson I'll stay right here."

Sally gave her a worried look. "You okay?"

"Fine."

A lie. She hadn't been fine. More coffee, more chocolate, and she'd tried not to think about the fact that as she sat obediently in her cubbyhole of an office, Jerry Simpson and His Highness, the Sheikh of Smugness, were probably enjoying a good laugh at her expense.

And why, she'd thought, should she let that happen? She could show her face, just to prove she might be down but she wasn't defeated.

So she'd combed her hair, straightened her panty hose, smoothed down the skirt of her navy suit and headed for the boardroom.

By the time she'd finally strolled in, the formal handshakes and greetings were over. Jerry Simpson saw her and glowered but what could he do about it without making a scene? The sheikh hadn't even noticed, surrounded as he was by his adoring fans and his pathetic minions.

Megan had tossed Jerry a thousand-watt smile meant to let him suffer as he tried to figure out why she'd showed up. Then she'd headed for the buffet table, where she'd sipped more coffee before switching to Mimosas.

No caffeine there. Only little bubbles.

All she had to do was hang in long enough to make Simpson squirm. Once the sheikh and his henchmen departed, she could start the ugly business of crawling back into her boss's good graces, though she doubted he'd let her get that far anytime this decade.

Well, no rush. The sheikh wasn't going anywhere. Not yet. Everyone was having too much fun. She could hear Jerry's voice, and a deeper, huskier one she assumed was the sheikh's. She could hear occasional trills of girlish laughter, too, punctuated by loud male ha-ha-ha's.

Like, for instance, right now. A giggle, a ha-ha, a simpering, "That's so clever, Your Highness!"

Megan swung around and stared at Geraldine McBride. Geraldine, simpering? All two hundred tweedy pounds of her?

Megan snorted.

She didn't mean to. She just couldn't help it, not while she was envisioning the Pooh-Bah riding an Arabian stallion with Geraldine flung across the saddle in front of him.

She snorted again. Unfortunately the second snort erupted during a second's pause in the babble of voices. Heads turned in her direction. Jerry looked as if he wanted to kill her. The sheikh looked—

Mmm-mmm-mmm. He looked spectacular. You had to give him that. The tabloids were right. The man was gorgeous. They had his eye-color wrong, though. It wasn't gray. The color reminded her of charcoal. Or slate.

Or storm clouds. That's how cold those eyes were as they fixed on her.

There was no mistaking that expression. He didn't like her. Not in the slightest. Jerry must have told him she'd been a problem.

So be it.

I don't like you, either, she thought coolly, and couldn't resist raising her glass in mocking salute before she turned away.

Why care what the sheikh thought? Why care what Jerry thought? Why care what anybody thought? She had her own life to live, her own independence to enjoy—

"Miss O'Connell," a deep voice said.

Megan swung around. The sheikh was coming toward her, his walk slow, deliberate and masculine enough to make her heart bump up into her throat, which was silly. There was nothing to be afraid of, except losing her job, and that wouldn't happen if she used her head.

He reached her side. Oh, yes. He was definitely easy on the eyes. Tall, lean, the hint of a well-muscled body under that expensive suit.

D and D, she thought, and her heart gave another little bump. What she and Bree always joked about.

Dark and Dangerous.

He gave her what the people at the other end of the room would surely think was a smile. It wasn't. That look in his eyes was colder than ever, cold enough to make the hair rise on the nape of her neck. How could such a gorgeous man be such a mean son of a bitch?

Megan drew herself up. "Your Mightiness."

His eyes bored into hers again. Then he lifted his hand. That was all. No wave, no turning around, nothing but that upraised hand. It was enough. Someone said something— her boss, maybe, or one of the sheikh's henchmen—and people headed for the door.

Scant seconds later, the room was empty.

Megan smiled sweetly. "Must be nice, being emperor of the universe."

"It must be equally nice, not caring what people think of you."

"I beg your pardon?"

His gaze moved over her, from her hair to her toes and then back up again. "You're drunk."

"I am not."

"Put down that glass."

Megan's eyebrows. "What?"

"I said, put the glass down."

"You can't tell me what to do."

"Someone should have told you what to do a long time ago," he said grimly. "Then you'd know better than to try to threaten me."

"Threaten you? Are you insane? I most assuredly did not—"

"For the last time, Miss O'Connell, put the glass down."

Megan's jaw shot forward. "For the last time, oh mighty king, stop trying to order me ar—"

Her words ended in a startled yelp as Sheikh Qasim al Daud al Rashid, King of Suliyam and Absolute Ruler of his People, picked her up, tossed her over his shoulder and marched from the room.

CHAPTER TWO

Caz hadn't intended to sling the O'Connell woman over his shoulder like a sack of grain.

He hadn't intended to deal with her at all. Oh, he wanted to, all right. Hell, yes, he wanted to. Simpson had told him how he'd given the woman a simple assignment, how she'd tried to make it seem as if he'd promised her something he hadn't...

And how she'd threatened to discredit him and Suliyam if she didn't get a job she wanted.

How dare she attempt to blackmail him?

He'd felt the rage churning inside him. His ancestors would have known how to deal with the woman.

Damn it, so did he.

Caz was the one who snorted now as he strode down the hall, past startled faces, the O'Connell woman beating her fists against his shoulders and yelling words a decent woman should not even think.

There was no need to go back to an earlier generation. Ninety percent of the men in Suliyam would know how to deal with her, and that was just the problem. After his hurried conversation with her boss, he'd known that if he let himself show his anger, he might as well put up a sign in Times Square that told the world he and his nation were still living in the dark ages.

So he'd decided to ignore her. There was no reason for

him to get involved. After all, Simpson said he'd made it clear to her that he was not going to give her the job.

"I took care of things, your highness," he'd said. "She's just one of those prickly feminists. You know the type."

Caz did, indeed. The western world was filled with them. They weren't soft-spoken or soft and welcoming, a safe harbor for a man who spent his days on the financial and political battlefields where empires were won and lost.

They were hard-edged and aggressive, unattractive and unfeminine.

He didn't enjoy their company. He certainly didn't understand them. Why would a woman want to behave like a man? But he'd learned not to underestimate their business skills, as long as they followed the rules.

If a woman wanted to play in a man's world, Caz expected her to play a man's game.

Threatening a lawsuit when none was warranted, pretending that things had been promised you when they hadn't, were things a woman would do.

Not a man.

Megan O'Connell slammed a fist between his shoulder blades. Caz grunted, stalked into Simpson's office and dumped her on a tweed-covered sofa. Then he stood back, folded his arms and glared at her.

She glared straight back. Didn't she have any sense of shame? Of guilt? Nobody glowered at him. Nobody! Didn't she realize who he was?

Of course she did. She just didn't care. He had to admire her courage.

He had to admire her looks, too. She didn't appear unfeminine, even in that shapeless blue suit. And she certainly wasn't unattractive, despite the blouse buttoned to the neck and the auburn hair tied back so tightly from her face that it made her sculpted cheekbones stand out like elegant arches. Her shoes were better suited to the legs of a soccer player than to ones that were so long, so artfully curved, so...

The woman sprang to her feet. "Who in hell do you think you are!"

"Sit down, Miss O'Connell."

"I will not sit down. I will not tolerate this kind of treatment." Eyes bright with anger, she started toward the door. "And I will not stay in this room with you for another—"

Caz kept his eyes on her as he reached back and slammed the door.

"I said, sit down."

"You have no authority here, mister! All I have to do is yell for help and—"

"And?" He smiled unpleasantly. "What will happen, Miss O'Connell? Do you really expect your boss to come running to your assistance after the threats you made?"

"What threats?" She folded her arms, lifted her chin and set one of those ugly shoes tapping with impatience. "I don't know what you're talking about.

Caz narrowed his eyes. Oh, yes. She was tough. She was also beautiful, but that didn't change a thing. She was prepared to ruin his plans for his country and his people for her own selfish purposes, and he would not tolerate it.

"Perhaps you'd like to tell me what threats I made."

"Don't waste my time, Miss O'Connell. The head of your office told me everything."

"Really." The foot-tapping increased in tempo. "And just what did he tell you?"

Caz's glower deepened. Simpson had told him more than enough to brand this woman as a schemer ready to lie and cheat and do whatever it took to get what she wanted, and what she wanted was the Suliyam account. She'd stop at nothing to get it, including threatening to file a lawsuit on the grounds that she was being discriminated against because of her sex.

"He explained what you said, your highness, that you cannot permit a woman to work alongside you."

Caz had never said any such thing. Not exactly. He'd simply explained that the status of women was an evolving issue in his country.

Simpson had assured him he understood. Obviously he hadn't. And now, Megan O'Connell was talking about hiring a lawyer.

Caz didn't give a damn about that. His attorneys would have the complaint dismissed without trouble. Suliyam's traditions were its own. No one could tell him or his people what to do or how to do it, not Megan O'Connell or all the lawyers and judges in the world.

Besides, the issue of her sex was secondary.

The woman was demanding a position for which she wasn't qualified. The man who'd actually created the proposal—someone named Fisher—was right for the job. His work had been excellent. It was the reason Caz had signed a contract with Tremont, Burnside and Macomb.

Megan O'Connell didn't have a legal leg to stand on. She knew it, too. Hadn't she admitted it to Simpson? You'd never win a lawsuit, Simpson said he'd told her, and she'd countered by saying she didn't care about winning.

Impugning Suliyam's name in the press and, worse still, in business and financial circles, would be enough for her.

Caz couldn't let that happen. Wouldn't let it happen. He'd spent the last five years readying his people for emergence from the past, but some among them would grasp any opportunity to end the progress he'd made. There were too many factions aligned against him. One whiff of scandal, one headline…

"Are you deaf, Sheikh Qasim? Or have you decided you made a mistake, conversing with a mere female?"

She was all but breathing fire now. Her face was flushed, her eyes were wide and dark; her hair was coming undone and tumbling around her face in wild curls. The suit and shoes were still ugly as sin but from the neck up, she looked like a woman who'd just risen from bed.

His bed.

The thought was unsettling. She was beautiful, yes, but her heart wasn't a woman's heart. She was intent on blackmail, and he was the target.

"It was your Mr. Simpson who made the mistake, Miss O'Connell, by letting things go too far."

Megan blinked. "What things?"

"It serves no purpose to pretend innocence." Caz folded his arms. "I told you, I know about your threats. Your Mr. Simpson—"

"He is not *my* anything!"

"He is your boss."

"He's a fool. So what?"

"He did what he could to keep the peace."

"Excuse me?"

"He was foolish to try. As soon as you began demanding undue credit for the little work you did, helping to draft that proposal—"

"Helping?" Megan gave a brittle laugh. "I *wrote* that proposal."

"No, you did not."

"Damn it!" Megan could almost feel the adrenaline racing through her veins. A couple of hours ago, she'd have voted Jerry Simpson Idiot of the Year. What a mistake that would have been. The barbarian barring the door was winner of the title, hands down. "You know what? I've had it.'' Resolutely she started toward the door again. "You get out of my way.''

He bared his teeth in a smile. "Or?'' he said pleasantly.

"Or I'll go right through you.''

He laughed. The son of a bitch laughed! Oh, how she wanted to slap that arrogant smirk from his all-too-perfect face.

Unfortunately, she could hardly blame him. Talk about empty threats! She could no more go through him than through a brick wall.

The Sheikh of the Endless Names was big. Six foot two, six foot three. He was as tall as any of her brothers and she'd never been able to go through them in a zillion touch football games. She'd hardly ever managed to go around them, except with a bit of subterfuge.

And then there were those shoulders wide enough to fill the doorway. The muscles that bulged even under his expensive suit. Except, they didn't bulge. They rippled.

Rippled? Megan did a mental blink. Who cared if his muscles undulated? The Prince of All He Surveyed was a male chauvinist jerk, and she'd be damned if she'd stand here and take his verbal abuse one more second.

"Perhaps it's the custom to detain women by force in your country,'' she said coldly.

That got a response! Red patches bloomed on his cheeks. The man didn't like hearing the truth. Good. She could use that to her advantage.

"Or maybe it's the only way you can get women to pay attention to you. You know, snatch them up, carry them off, lock them up—''

"You're trying my patience, Miss O'Connell.''

"And you're trying mine.''

"I promise you, I won't take much more.''

"And I promise *you*—''

That was as far as she got. He reached for her, wrapped his hands around her arms and lifted her to her toes. His fingers pressed into her flesh and his eyes… Whoa, his eyes! Cold as that sea-ice again. He was angry. Enraged. Megan could see it, feel it, even smell his fury in the male musk coming off him.

She'd never seen or sensed such passion in a man before. *What would he be like in bed?*

The thought shocked her. She didn't think about men that way. Oh, she could joke with her sisters, sit in a bar sipping a glass of white wine and giggle with them over the buns on one guy, the biceps on the next, but she'd never looked at a man and actually wondered what it would be like to sleep with him.

That was exactly what she was doing now.

What if the sheikh turned all that rage into desire? If he were lying above her, holding her this same way, holding her so she couldn't turn away from him, so she didn't want to turn away from him, so she could feel the heat of his body against hers?

She felt her heart do a slow, unsteady roll.

"Let go," she said, and thanked whatever gods were watching that her voice didn't tremble.

He didn't. Not right away. He went on looking at her and her heart did that same little turn again because something changed in his eyes and she knew he was thinking the same thing, seeing her as she saw him, not here in this office but in a wide, soft bed, their bodies slick with sweat, their mouths fused.

Her pulse went crazy—but not as crazy as that thought.

"I said, let go!" she repeated, and twisted free of his hands.

A moment passed. She could hear the rasp of his breath.

Then his expression changed and it was as if nothing had happened.

"This isn't getting us anywhere," he said.

Megan nodded. "I agree."

"Fifty thousand dollars."

She blinked. "What?"

"Fifty thousand, Miss O'Connell. Surely that's ample payment for the time you'd like me to think you put in on this project."

She stared at him in disbelief. "Are you offering me a bribe?"

"I'm offering you payment for the job you claim to have done."

"My God, you are! You think you can buy my silence!"

His eyes darkened. "Let's not make a melodrama out of this. You've threatened to derail a project that's of great importance to me. I'm simply suggesting there's no need for you to do that." He smiled, and she wanted to wipe the smile off his face. "I don't carry a checkbook with me, of course—"

"Of course."

"But I will have a courier deliver a check to you here within—"

"No!"

"Ah. You'd rather we kept the transaction private." He reached in his breast pocket, took out a small leather notebook and a pen. "If you'll give me your home address—"

"I am not for sale, Sheikh Qasim!"

Caz looked up. The woman's face was white, except for two slashes of crimson across those elegant cheekbones. She was going to be more difficult to deal with than he'd anticipated.

"How much?" he said coldly.

"I just told you, I am not—"

"One hundred thousand."

"Are you deaf? I said—"

"I'm weary of this game, Miss O'Connell, and of your act. Name your price."

She laughed. Laughed! At him! And edged toward the door, still laughing, as if he were a lunatic howling at the moon.

"Goodbye, your Mightiness. It's been interest—"

She gasped as he grabbed her shoulders and swung her toward him.

"How dare you laugh at me?" he growled.

"Take your hands off me."

"You're a fool, Miss O'Connell. Did you really think you could threaten me and get away with it?"

Megan looked up into eyes filled with hostility. She knew that this was the moment to tell the sheikh that her threat, as he called it, had been made in the heat of the moment, that there'd be no lawsuit because Simpson, damn his soul, was right. The only thing she'd win, if she sued, was a reputation as a troublemaker, and that would mark the end of her corporate career.

That was the logical thing to do.

Logic, however, had nothing to do with what she felt at that moment.

The sheikh obviously thought he ruled the universe. Well, why wouldn't he? During her research, she'd learned that women were treated like dirt in his country. Well, she was a woman, but she didn't have to bow to this man. She was an American citizen, and she didn't have to take this nonsense.

"I asked you a question," he said. "Did you think—"

"What I think," Megan said, enunciating each word with precision, "is that you're a tyrant. You're so used to people treating you like a god, to *you* treating *them* as if they were your property—''

"Stop it! How dare you?"

"What you mean," she said, her voice trembling, "is how dare a woman speak to you this way? Isn't that right, Sheikh Qasim? I'm a female. A worthless creature. And you are absolutely certain that women are only good for one thing."

Caz could feel the anger rushing through him. Control, he told himself, control…but this woman needed a lesson.

"It's time somebody showed you what women really are," she said, and those few words pushed him over the edge.

"At least we agree on something," he answered, and before she could twist her head away, his mouth came down over hers.

His kiss was harsh. Dominating. He was a man intent on proving his strength and her weakness, his power to subdue her.

Megan fought back. Hard. When he tried to open her mouth with his, she sank her teeth into his bottom lip. He grunted, turned, pushed her back against the wall; she shoved against his chest, freed her hands, beat them against his shoulders…

And then, in a heartbeat, it all changed.

Later, she'd think back and remember the sudden stillness in the room, as if the universe was holding its breath. Now all she knew was the feel of his mouth as it softened on hers, the gentling of his hands as they slid up her shoulders, her throat, into her hair.

It was happening again. What she'd felt minutes ago, except now it was real. She was in his arms, her body pressed to his, and what was happening had everything to do with desire instead of anger, with wanting instead of hating.

She moaned, parted her lips to the feathery brush of his tongue, let him take possession of her mouth. Of her senses.

He said something in a language she didn't understand, but it didn't matter. She understood all the rest. What he wanted. What she wanted, and when he angled his mouth over hers, took the kiss deeper and deeper until she felt the earth spinning away, Megan raised her arms, wound them around his neck. He ran a hand down her spine, cupped her bottom, lifted her into him, into his heat, his hardness…

Someone knocked at the door. The sound was like a clap of thunder exploding within the confines of the quiet room.

Caz's hands fell away from her. He stepped back; her eyes flew open. Breathing hard, they stared at each other like partners who'd lost their footing in some intricate dance.

The knock at the door sounded again. A voice called out. It took Caz seemingly endless seconds to realize it was Hakim, calling his name.

"Sire? Sire, forgive me for disturbing you…"

Caz stared at the O'Connell woman. What in hell had just happened? A shared hallucination? An aberration? His gaze hardened. There were those among his people who would say she was not just a liar and a cheat but a sorceress. He knew better. She was only a woman. A seductive woman, and he'd played right into her hands.

Perhaps she thought she could sleep her way into the job she wanted, rather than blackmail her way into it. Or that she could use the last few minutes against him, either in a court of law or in ways that had the potential to be even more damaging.

He could almost see the headlines in the *Wall Street Journal.* Wouldn't his enemies love it if she denounced him to the press?

"Sire?"

She was still staring at him, her green eyes huge and seemingly clouded with confusion. If nothing else, she was an excellent actress.

Caz forced a smile to his lips. "Thank you for the taste of your wares, but you're wasting your time. I'm not interested."

"You arrogant son of a bitch!" Her face went white and she raised her hand, swung her fist at his jaw, but he slipped the punch with ease, caught her wrist and dragged her hard against him.

"Be careful," he said softly, "or before you know it, you'll be in water so deep it will be over your head."

"Don't you ever, *ever,* touch me again!"

A chilling smile angled across his mouth. "That's the first thing you've said that pleases me." He let go of her, took a breath to compose himself and opened the door. Hakim stood just outside, his expression as inscrutable as always.

"What is it, Hakim?"

"I am sorry to trouble you, my lord, but you told me to remind you of your luncheon appointment."

Caz nodded. He had not told Hakim any such thing, but his *aide de camp* had served first his father and now him. The man had a sixth sense about trouble, and the courage to act on his own initiative when he thought it necessary.

There were times it was an annoyance, but right now, Caz was glad he had.

"Yes. Thank you." He shot a glance at Megan O'Connell. She had turned away from him and was standing by the window, back straight, hands in the pockets of her mannish skirt, looking out at the street as if nothing had happened, but then, nothing had.

This had been a momentary slip in the fabric of time. Nothing more. It surely would never be repeated. Not only didn't she appeal to him; he would never see her again.

"A courier will deliver the item we discussed to your home this evening, Miss O'Connell."

The sheikh's voice was brisk and businesslike. Megan knotted her hands. Flying across the room and beating her fists against that arrogant face would serve no purpose. Besides, he'd never let it happen. He was too strong, far stronger than she. Hadn't he just proved it by overpowering her? Because that was what he'd done. Overpowered her. He'd forced that kiss on her, forced her to kiss him back...

"Are you going to give me your address? Or shall my aide get it from Simpson?"

She didn't answer. She didn't trust herself to speak. Let him send a check to her apartment. Let him send a dozen checks. She'd make the courier wait while she tore them into thousands of pieces and tell him precisely what he was to tell the sheikh to do with all those bits of paper.

At least she'd have the satisfaction of knowing his Mightiness would spend sleepless nights worrying that she'd sue. With luck, he'd have an ulcer by the time he finally realized she wouldn't.

"Miss O'Connell?"

Megan turned around. "Get out of my sight."

Caz stiffened. He heard Hakim make a sound that might have been a growl as he took a step forward.

"No," Caz said sharply, putting his hand on his aide's shoulder.

"But my lord..."

"She's American," Caz said, because that explained everything.

"Damned right I am," Megan said. "And you're a pig."

He forced a smile to his lips, as if she'd handed him a compliment.

"Goodbye, Miss O'Connell. You'll see my courier this evening." He moved toward her and was gratified to see the swift rush of panic in her eyes. "But for your sake," he said softly, so softly that he knew Hakim couldn't hear him, "you'd better pray that you never see me again."

The sheikh turned on his heel and strode from the room. His aide gave Megan one last, menacing look, then fell in after him.

Megan drew a shuddering breath and sank into a chair. The Prince of the Desert was gone. He was out of her life, forever.

And not a moment too soon.

CHAPTER THREE

MEGAN left work at six-thirty, almost an hour later than usual.

Since she'd expected to be quick-marched out of the building after her confrontation with the sheikh, leaving late wasn't too bad.

To her surprise, Simpson hadn't fired her. Either he'd believed her lawsuit threat or...

Or what?

She was glad she still had her job, but she couldn't figure out the reason.

Megan sighed as she stepped from the elevator.

Actually she couldn't figure out much of anything anymore, including why she'd never even imagined she could win a legal battle. Not that she regretted anything she'd said to either Simpson or Sheikh Qasim. It was just that nothing seemed quite as black and white as it had hours before.

Rain was beating against the glass lobby doors. Great. The weatherman had predicted overcast skies. How come those guys never got it right?

How come *she* hadn't? Megan asked herself as she turned up her collar and stepped into the street.

Threatening to sue had sounded good. Telling the sheikh what she thought of him had felt good. Great...except, all she'd really done was commit professional suicide. Odds were she'd be digging through the employment ads by next week.

A gust of wind blew the chill rain into her face. Too bad something like that hadn't happened hours earlier. She could have used an icy dousing around then.

Tremont, Burnside and Macomb was a prestigious firm. So what if her boss was an ass? That didn't change the facts. She'd behaved stupidly, first with her boss, then with her client...

Except, the sheikh wasn't her client, and that was probably a good thing because she never could have worked with him. How could you work with a man who was so obnoxious? So rude? So over-bearing and demanding and arrogant?

How could you work with a man who kissed you and turned your bones to jelly?

Megan reached the parking lot, unlocked her car and tossed her briefcase and purse on the passenger seat. She slid behind the wheel, started the engine and turned up the heat. She was drenched and her teeth were chattering.

There was no sense in lying to herself. Qasim had kissed her and she'd kissed him back. It had only been a kiss, but it had left her breathless. Who knew what might have happened if his aide hadn't interrupted them?

She swallowed hard and stared through the rain-streaked windshield. The other cars were blurs of color.

That was how she'd felt when they'd kissed. As if the world had disappeared and only the colors of it remained.

Damn it.

She gave herself a little shake, turned on the windshield wipers and headed into the street.

She'd absolutely made a mess of things, from start to finish. Too much caffeine. Okay, too much caffeine and too little common sense. She shouldn't have lost her temper and backed herself into a figurative corner.

And she shouldn't have been such an easy target for a

man who undoubtedly thought women were for only one thing.

The truth was that nothing would have happened if Hakim or Akim, whatever the Head Flunky's name was, hadn't shown up.

"Nothing at all," she muttered, and pulled out into traffic, which was even more horrible than usual. Well, why not? An extra hour spent creeping home on slick roads would be the perfect ending to a perfect day.

Her life was starting to feel like a soap opera.

She hit every red light between the parking lot and the freeway entrance ramp. Okay, she thought, drumming her fingers against the steering wheel. That gave her plenty of time to try and figure out why Simpson hadn't dumped her.

Could he really have fallen for the lawsuit thing?

No. The Worm was a rat and if that was a mixed metaphor, so be it. The point was, rats were miserable creatures but they weren't stupid. Her boss had seen through her threat.

He had to know that she wouldn't go to the media, either. Any action she took that would tarnish the company and the sheikh would tarnish her.

Goodbye, career. Goodbye, all these years spent climbing the corporate ladder.

Simpson had to know she'd calm down and come to her senses.

But the sheikh had no way of knowing it. He'd fall for anything she said. Obviously he had. That was the reason he'd made that loathsome offer to buy her off.

Had he gone to Simpson? Told her boss not to worry, that he had things under control? Was that why Simpson hadn't fired her, or even come near her for the balance of the day?

Maybe so.

Well, they were both in for a big surprise. Just let His Almightiness try and send her a check. Just let the Worm try to think she could be bought off. Just let...

"Stop," Megan said firmly. "Just stop." She was working herself up all over again, and for what? She'd already decided what to do with a check, if the sheikh sent one. As for Simpson... She wouldn't let him buy her off, either. To hell with the big Hollywood client. To hell with the partnership. She'd polish up her résumé, call up a headhunter, find herself a new job...

And lose the chance to make partner. Simpson saw it as a bribe but she deserved it. She was a hard worker. An excellent financial analyst. Was she really going to let Simpson and the insufferable Qasim of Suliyam make her lose everything she'd striven for?

She was not.

If she could just come up with the reason for Simpson's silence...

Her cell phone rang. Megan ignored it. She hated taking calls when she was driving, especially in heavy traffic made even worse by a steady rain. Whoever it was would call back. Or leave a message. Or—

Or be as persistent as an ant at a picnic. The phone rang again. And again. The fourth time, she kept her eyes on the wet road and dug the phone from her purse.

"This better be important," she said, "because I am knee-deep in rain and traffic and—"

"Megan?"

"Yes?" she said cautiously. It was a male voice, familiar, but she couldn't quite place it.

"Thank God," the voice said, and sighed with relief. "It's Frank."

"Who?"

"Frank Fisher. From the office."

"Frank?" Her mind buzzed with questions. Why was he calling her? And why did he sound so…panicked?

"Look, I hate to bother you, but—but, uh, I guess Mr. Simpson spoke to you about, uh, about things."

Mr. Simpson? Her eyes narrowed. "If you mean, did he tell me that you're stealing my work and claiming it as your own, yes. He spoke to me about, uh, things."

"Hey. I didn't steal anything. This wasn't my idea, it was Mr. Simpson's."

Oh, hell. Frank was right, it wasn't his fault. It would have been nice if he'd spoken up and told the Worm he wouldn't take credit for something that wasn't his, but Frank was spineless. Everyone in the office knew it. Intelligent, but spineless. Simpson had chosen him wisely.

"Forget it," she said wearily.

"I was hoping you'd say that."

A horn bleated behind her. She looked in the mirror, saw, through the water racing down the rear window, a small, low, obscenely expensive sports car. Typically L.A., and no doubt driven by a typically L.A. jerk who thought the car would make him look more important than he really was. She couldn't see the driver, thanks to the rain, but she didn't have to. She knew the type.

"Yeah, well, it's good of you to call, Frank. I mean, the apology doesn't change anything, but—"

"The apology?" Frank cleared his throat. "Uh, right, right. I'm glad you understand but actually—actually, I called to ask you something."

Megan frowned. "What?"

"Well," Frank said, and paused. "Well, see, I was reading through your—through my—through the proposal—"

Megan felt the blood start to drum in her ears. "Get to it, Frank. What do you want?"

"There are a couple of things here I don't quite follow…"

Frank began to babble. A couple of minutes later, it was clear there were lots of things he didn't follow. Like, for instance, the entire purpose of her suggestions for the investments the sheikh was seeking.

"He's rich, right?"

"Stinking rich," Megan agreed.

"And they've already got oil coming out of the faucets in Suminan, right?"

"Suliyam. Yes, the oil's pumping. But there's more to be found, and there are minerals in the mountains…"

And what was she doing, giving Frank a quick education based on her research? The man was an idiot. Why should she help him? Damn it, the jerk behind her was beeping his horn again.

"What?" she snarled, shooting an angry look in the mirror. Did Mr. Impatient expect her to fly over the cars ahead of her?

"I need answers, Megan. That's what."

"I wasn't talking to you, Frank."

"Yeah, but I need answers." Frank's voice cracked. "And soon. I'm meeting the sh—I'm meeting my client in less than an hour and, like I said, I just took a quick look at this proposal and—"

"And you're in over your head," Megan said sweetly, and hit the disconnect button so forcefully she thought she might have broken it.

The phone rang a second later. She ignored it. It rang again, and she grabbed the phone, shut it off and, for good measure, tossed it over her shoulder into the back seat.

This was why Simpson hadn't fired her.

He needed her. All that crap about her staying in L.A. to assist Fisher was just that. Crap. She was going to stay here and force-feed everything to her replacement. Frank would get the scepter. She'd get the shaft.

"Forget it," she snapped.

No way was she going to take that kind of treatment. What was with men, anyway? Three of them had tried to step on her today. Simpson. Fisher. And the sheikh.

"Don't forget the sheikh, Megan," she said out loud, but how could she possibly forget a man so despicable?

He'd kissed her. So what? It was a kiss. That was all, just a kiss. Okay, so he was good at it. Damned good, but why wouldn't he be when he'd been with a zillion women? That was what he did. Made love to women, ordered his flunkies around, and sat on his butt the rest of the time, counting his money, figuring out ways to make it grow.

What else would a rich, incredibly good-looking Prince of the Desert do with his life?

To think that such a man believed he could buy her...

The idiot behind her hit his horn again. This time, it was a long, long blast that seemed to go on forever.

Megan looked in the mirror.

"Go on," she snarled, "pass me if you can, you idiot!"

The horn blared again. Megan cursed, put down her window just enough so she could stick out her hand and make the universal sign of displeasure. She'd never done such a thing before in her life but oh, it felt good!

The driver behind her swung out, horn blasting in answer to her gesture. He cut in front of her, then put on the speed and zoomed away, in and out of the smallest possible breaks in traffic until he vanished from sight.

"Are you really in such an all-fired hurry to get to hell?" she yelled.

Then she put up her window, glared straight ahead and wished nothing but life's worst on the Worm, the Sheikh, Frank Fisher, and the idiot driving the Lamborghini.

*   *   *

California drivers were not only fools, they were foolhardy.

The mood he was in, Caz had half a mind to force the VW onto the shoulder of the freeway, yank open the driver's door and tell the cretin behind the wheel that making a crude gesture to a stranger wasn't a good idea.

Luckily for the cretin, he was in a hurry.

The traffic had been bumper to bumper. When it finally loosened up, he'd waited for the guy ahead to start moving. He hadn't. Or maybe she hadn't. Caz had pretty much generated a picture of who was behind the VW's wheel. A woman. Middle-aged, peering over the steering wheel with trepidation, nervous about the rain.

The finger-in-the-air thing had changed his mind.

No gray-haired Nervous Nellie would make such a gesture. She wouldn't yap on a cell phone while she was driving, either. At least, he thought he'd seen the driver holding a cell phone to her ear. It was hard to tell much of anything because of the rain, and who was it who'd said it never rained in Southern California?

Hell.

He had to calm down.

Driving fast would help. It always did. It was what he did at the end of virtually every meeting with his advisors back home, take one of his cars out on the straight black road that went from one end of Suliyam to the other.

From no place to nowhere, his mother used to say.

Caz always thought of her when he was in California. She'd left his father and come here, where she'd been born, when he was ten. She died when he was twelve, and he'd only spent summers with her for the intervening two years.

"Won't you come home with me, Mama?" he'd ask at the end of each summer. And she'd hug him tightly and say she'd come home soon...

But she never did.

He'd hated her for a little while, when he was thirteen or fourteen and Hakim let slip that she'd left his father and him because she'd despised living in Suliyam. He hadn't known that. His father had always told him his mother had gone back to her beloved California for a holiday, that she'd taken ill and had to stay there to get the proper medical care.

It turned out only part of that was true. She'd gotten sick and died in California, all right, but she hadn't gone for a holiday. She'd abandoned everything. Her husband, her adopted country...

Her son.

Caz frowned, saw an opening in the next lane and shot into it.

It had all happened more than twenty years ago. Water under the bridge, as the Americans said.

He had more important things to think about.

Caz sighed. He was wound up like a spring about to-night's dinner appointment. He had to relax. That woman was to blame for his bad mood. What an aggressive female! A feminist, to the core.

Was that the genie in the bottle he'd be setting loose, once he began implementing his plans back home? Maybe, and maybe he'd regret it, but you couldn't lead a nation into the twenty-first century without granting rights and privileges to all its citizens.

Even women.

Surely they wouldn't all turn out like...

No. He wasn't going to think about Megan O'Connell. He'd wasted too much time on her already. All in all, this day had been a mess.

First that abominable meeting this morning. He'd taken one look at the buffet table, the champagne, the people star-

ing at him and he'd been tempted to turn and walk out. He
hadn't, of course. He was his nation's emissary. Manners,
protocol, were everything.

How come he'd forgotten that with the woman? He'd lost
it with her and he knew it but, damn it, she'd deserved it.
That temper. Those threats...

*Those eyes, that mouth, the certainty that the body be-
neath the awful suit was meant for pleasure...*

"Hell," Caz said, and stepped harder on the gas.

Business. That was what he had to concentrate on tonight.

It was what he'd wanted to concentrate on this morning,
but Simpson had screwed it up. Instead of serious discussion
with the man who'd written that excellent proposal, he'd
had to endure an eternity of all those people fawning over
him.

Bad enough his own countrymen insisted on treating him
as if he were Elvis risen from the dead. That, at least, was
understandable. It was tradition, the same tradition, unchanged for centuries, that would make implementing his plans
a rough sell. His advisors would look aghast at his deter-
mination to create a modern infrastructure in Suliyam by
opening it to foreign investors. He intended to commit much
of his own vast fortune to the plan, as well.

His people would balk, protest, tell him such things could
not be done.

It was tradition.

And it was tradition, too, that said he could not possibly
bring a woman into Suliyam as his financial advisor.

He had explained all of that to Simpson from the first.
He knew there were bright, well-educated women in the
west. Hadn't his mother been one of them? But Suliyam
wasn't ready for such things. He supposed it was one of the
reasons his parents' marriage had fallen apart.

He hadn't told that to Simpson, of course, but he'd made

it clear he would not be able to work with anyone but a man.

"No problem, your worship," Simpson had said.

"I am not called by that title," Caz had told him pleasantly. "Please, just address me as Sheikh Qasim."

Hakim had given him a look that meant he didn't approve. Caz had ignored him. Hakim was devoted and loyal, but he believed in the old ways and those days were coming to an end.

"I will assign my best person to write this proposal, your majesty," Simpson had replied.

Caz put on his signal light and shot across three lanes of traffic to the exit ramp.

He'd given up correcting the little man. What did it matter how Simpson addressed him as long as he found the right man to get the job done?

He had. The proposal was everything Caz had hoped for and more. He'd searched hard for the right firm to handle the account, narrowed his choices to three and asked them to come up with written proposals for the best possible utilization of investment funds in Suliyam.

Three months later, each company had submitted a fine proposal. Still, making the final decision had been easy. The T S and M report stood head and shoulders above the others. Caz knew he'd found his man.

Simpson was an annoyance, but Frank Fisher, whose name was on the proposal, was brilliant. He was the right person for the job: logical, methodical, pragmatic.

All the things Megan O'Connell wasn't.

The woman was a creature of temper and temperament, all blistering heat one moment and bone-chilling ice the next. Their encounter proved, as if proof were necessary, that she could not possibly have written the document in question.

It took no great genius to figure out that Simpson was right about her.

She'd accept the money Caz had offered and be grateful for it. The thought of paying her off infuriated him, but sometimes the old saying was right. Better to placate the occasional jackal than to lose the entire flock.

Caz glanced at his watch. Almost seven. He was meeting Fisher for dinner. He hadn't intended to bother with such a meeting—Fisher was making the flight to Suliyam with him tomorrow, so there'd be plenty of time to talk—but Fisher hadn't been present this morning. He was tying up loose ends on another account, Simpson said.

No problem, Caz had answered.

But he'd reconsidered. He really did want to meet Fisher as soon as possible. There was always the faint chance they wouldn't hit it off. If Fisher were anything like Simpson, for instance. If Caz intimidated him simply by being there, they'd never be able to work together.

That was one thing about Megan O'Connell. She damned well hadn't been intimidated. She'd treated him as if he was a man, not a prince. She'd kissed him that way...

Enough.

He had to clear his mind for the meeting ahead. He'd set it up only a little while ago, on the phone with Simpson.

"I'd like to have dinner with Mr. Fisher this evening," he'd said.

Well, that might be difficult to arrange, Simpson had replied. It was late in the day. Fisher wasn't in the office. He might not be able to make a meeting called at the last moment.

"I'll expect him to meet me at seven," Caz had said, cutting through the excuses.

A more suspicious man might even think Simpson was trying to keep him from meeting Frank Fisher until it was too late, but that was ridiculous. Simpson would want Fisher to be on his toes for their first encounter. Meeting this way, after the man had put in a day's work, might not be the best time for him to shine.

Why else would Simpson sound nervous? Surely not because he didn't think Fisher couldn't handle questions on the fine points and subtle implications of the proposal he'd drafted.

The O'Connell woman wasn't capable of such complex work. Simpson had laughed at the very idea. Caz had come to that same conclusion on his own. She was a brash, fiery redhead whose talents lay in a very different direction than finance.

And he'd kissed her.

Her taste lingered on his lips, her scent in his nostrils. He could almost feel the softness of her breasts against his chest, the delicate tilt of her pelvis against him.

Damn it. He was turning hard, just thinking about that kiss.

Why? Why had he kissed her? He didn't like her. What man would like a woman who threatened his plans?

Sure, some men didn't have to like a woman to want to bed her, but he wasn't one of those men. The papers printed lies about him as a womanizer. He'd long ago given up protesting because the protests only added fuel to the fire.

The truth was, he never slept with a woman unless he found her interesting and intelligent.

Megan O'Connell was interesting and intelligent, but she was also a liar. He didn't want to sleep with her.

No, he didn't.

Caz muttered a word he'd learned not in Suliyam but in the American university he'd attended. The restaurant where he was to meet Fisher was just ahead. He'd been there before, always without his entourage. It was a small place with good food where nobody recognized him or bothered him.

That made it perfect for tonight. A pleasant meal with the man who'd written that excellent proposal... Yes. He was looking forward to it.

Caz pulled into the lot behind the restaurant, parked the Lamborghini and told himself, with relief, that there was no reason for him to think of Megan O'Connell ever again.

CHAPTER FOUR

MEGAN saw the red light on her answering machine blinking as she let herself into her apartment, but she ignored it.

She didn't want to hear another human voice, not tonight. All she wanted right now was to turn the long, awful day into a memory.

Like a snake shedding its suddenly constricting skin, she kicked off her sensible shoes, tossed her rain-soaked jacket on a chair, unzipped her soggy skirt and peeled off her silk blouse, her bra and pantyhose. She unpinned her hair, filled the tub, dumped in a handful of lemon-scented bath salts and sank into the warm, fragrant water.

Sheer bliss.

For the first time all day, she began to feel human.

Half an hour later, wearing old sweats that dated back to her university days and a pair of fuzzy slippers even older than the sweats, she padded into the kitchen and flicked on the light.

The answering machine was still blinking. According to the red dial on its face, four messages were waiting for her now. So what? She wasn't doing anything she didn't absolutely have to do tonight, and that included blow-drying and endlessly brushing her hair to make it straight.

Let it be a curly mop. Tomorrow was Saturday. She didn't have to worry about leaping out of bed at six and turning herself into Megan O'Connell, girl financial whiz. No need to dress-for-success or brace herself for another encounter with Jerry Simpson. What for? Her days of striving for success were over. Come Monday, she'd either be fired or get a big, fat, juicy new client.

All she could do was wait and see which way things went, though she had a feeling that hanging up on Frank a little while ago had kind of settled the issue.

Megan opened the fridge, took a slightly shriveled carrot stick from a plastic bag and bit down on it.

And it was all the sheikh's fault.

"The rat," she said, and tossed the half-eaten carrot into the trash.

Time to stop thinking about *el sheikh-o*. Time to dump him in the trash along with the carrot stick. Time to purge her mind of the miserable memories of the miserable day. Forget Simpson. Forget Frank Fisher. Forget Qasim the Horrible and the fact that she'd let him kiss her.

People under stress did weird things, and heaven knew she'd been under stress.

She'd concentrate on something positive. Something like dinner. An excellent idea. She was starved, and why wouldn't she be? Thanks to the sheikh, she'd skipped breakfast and lunch, spending the one getting ready for his visit and the other recovering from it...

And there he was, inside her head again.

Out with thoughts of the sheikh. In with thoughts about supper. Comfort food. That was what she wanted, something as homey and warming as the bath and the old sweat suit.

Megan opened the refrigerator again, her spirits sinking as she peered inside. Low-fat yogurt. Low-fat cottage cheese. Three little containers of low-fat pudding that was supposed to taste like the real thing and didn't.

Damn.

She didn't want anything sensible tonight. She wanted something like her mother's fantastic rice pudding, or a big bowl of macaroni and cheese, anything with enough built-in calories to soothe the soul in every delicious, decadent mouthful.

She sighed, shut the refrigerator door and leaned back against it. She didn't have macaroni in the pantry, and her mother was hundreds of miles away in Las Vegas, so there'd be no rice pudding tonight. A good thing, too, because how would she ever have explained to Ma that she needed it because she'd managed to let a man she despised turn her on?

Qasim hadn't just turned her on, he'd turned her inside out.

Damned if she'd let that ruin her weekend.

Forget the cottage cheese, the yogurt, the sheikh. A little Thai takeout place had opened around the corner a couple of weeks ago. They'd tucked menus in all the mail boxes and she'd put hers somewhere…

There it was, stuck to the fridge door with a magnet.

Megan read through the specials. Great. Coconut milk soup. Pad Thai with chicken. Sticky rice. It wasn't Ma's rice pudding or her own mac and cheese but it sounded wonderful. It probably *was* comfort food, if you were Thai.

She smiled for what felt like the first time in a century. Tonight, she'd claim honorary citizenship. Still smiling, she reached for the phone…

Someone rang the doorbell.

She looked up, frowning. Who'd drop over at this hour on such a wet, cold night?

The sheikh's courier, that was who. Her smile disappeared as she dropped the telephone. She'd told him what he could do with his money but that hadn't stopped him and now one of his rain-soaked flunkies, probably Hakim of the icy eyes, was at the door with one hundred thousand bucks in his pocket.

Pin money, to a man who owned a couple of dozen oil wells. A fortune to her, and he knew it.

He figured she'd leap at it like a dog jumping for a bone.

Bzzz bzzz bzzz.

The flunky was impatient. Megan's eyes narrowed. Right. So was she. How many times did a woman have to say "no?"

The almighty prince needed a lesson. What better than to see his check shredded into as many bits as there were raindrops pattering against the roof? Even a thick-skulled despot would get that message.

Bzzz bzzz bzzz bzzz.

Megan grabbed a pair of scissors from a pottery jug filled with kitchen tools and hurried to the door. Bristling with anger, she flung it open.

"Doing your master's bidding, are you, Mr. Hakim? Okay. It's time I showed you and him what he can do with—with—"

Her eyes widened. It wasn't Hakim on the tiny porch.

"Such a warm greeting," the sheikh said. His gaze fell to the scissors clutched in her hand. A wry smile tilted across his mouth. "Do your always greet your guests with shears in your hand?"

"What the hell are you doing here?"

"At the moment, I'm standing in the rain."

"You know what I mean. How did you get my address?"

"I'll be happy to answer your questions, Miss O'Connell, but not while I'm drowning."

She almost laughed at the sight of the man standing beneath the steady stream of water pouring from the sagging rain gutter. Her landlord had ignored her complaints about it.

Now, she was glad he had.

"Consider it a bonus for turning up unannounced," she

said sweetly. "What's the matter? Don't you trust your henchman with your money?"

"You're wrong about Hakim."

"And you're wrong in thinking I've changed my mind about taking your bribe."

Good. That sent a little shot of color into his face. "I haven't come here to offer you money, Miss O'Connell."

"And I'm not going to let you in. So, goodbye, your highness. Seems to me, that concludes our bus—"

"We have things to discuss."

"You're wrong. It's late, and you have nothing to say that would interest me."

"It is late, yes. As for what I might say that would change your mind…" Caz took a deep breath. "How about, 'I was wrong?'"

"Look, your highness… What did you say?"

Caz cleared his throat. A little while ago, he'd thought nothing could taste as bad as the bitterness of the food he'd eaten with Frank Fisher. He'd been wrong. Humble pie tasted a hell of a lot worse.

"Wrong about what?"

"I may have misjudged you." Wrong choice of words. He saw her reaction in her eyes. "All right," he said quickly, I *did* misjudge you. Now, do you think you could stand aside and let me step into your living room before I go down for the third time?"

He smiled, but he didn't mean it. Megan could see the banked anger in his eyes. What had happened? Why was he here?

There was only one way to find out. She stepped back and motioned him inside.

"You have five minutes."

"Thank you."

The "thank you" had all the sincerity of a cobra thanking a mouse for agreeing to dinner. What was going on here?

"Do you think you could put those scissors aside?"

"Why?" Megan smiled thinly. "Do they make you nervous?"

"Perhaps we can sit down, like civilized people."

"Me at your feet?"

"Miss O'Connell. I understand that you're angry—"

"Me?" Megan slammed the door, strode past Qasim and tossed the scissors on a table. "Don't be silly. What possible reason would I have for being angry?"

"I suppose I should have called first."

"Yes, you should. You'd have saved yourself a trip." She folded her arms. Her heart was beating as fast as a hummingbird's wings. Well, why wouldn't it? It surely had nothing to do with the way he looked, tall and incredibly handsome with drops of rain glittering like diamonds in his dark hair. "What's the problem, your highness? Why would you possibly think you'd misjudged me?" She smiled tightly. "Last I saw, you and your flunky had me all figured out."

"Hakim isn't anybody's flunky. He's an old and trusted friend."

"Friends don't click their heels and salute."

"Hakim does neither."

"A matter of opinion."

"A matter of fact." Caz ground his teeth together. Why was he letting her sidetrack him? Bad enough he'd had to beg to come in out of the rain, that he was going to have to plead for forgiveness. Did he have to take this woman's insults, too?

Yes, he thought glumly, he did. He was, as the Americans said, stuck between a rock and a hard place. Megan O'Connell had an attitude problem. Thanks to her employer's duplicity, he was going to have to get used to dealing with it.

Caz forced a smile to his lips.

"I haven't come to talk about Hakim."

"No?"

"No. As I said, I came to tell you I misjudged you."

Her eyes flashed. "Stop dancing around the subject, your highness. Say what you mean."

"I had dinner with Frank Fisher."

"And? What's the problem. Did Frank eat his peas with a spoon?"

He took a quick step forward. Megan's breath caught, but she stood her ground.

"I warn you," he said softly, "I'm not in a good mood."

"Good. Neither am I. I take it your meal didn't go well."

"It was fine, until I began discussing the proposal." Caz's eyes darkened. "Mr. Fisher tried to change the subject."

Megan folded her arms. "I'll bet he did."

"I was persistent, at which point he excused himself and went to the men's room." Caz smiled coldly. "He went to the men's room a number of times over the next few minutes."

"Ah. Well, maybe the food you'd eaten didn't agree with him."

"The conversation didn't agree with him. The last time he left the table, I followed him. He didn't go to the men's room, Miss O'Connell, he went to make a phone call. In fact, I'm sure he'd made several phone calls." He shot a pointed look at the blinking light on Megan's answering machine. "But the person he was trying to reach wasn't home…or wasn't interested in taking his calls."

"Why don't I save us both some time, Sheikh Qasim? You wanted to talk about the Suliyam proposal. Frank didn't. Maybe I should say he couldn't, because he doesn't know the first thing about it.''

"That's correct. And after some pointed questioning, he told me everything. That you'd written it, not he. That Simpson had promised you'd stay in the States and feed him whatever information he might need.''

"And that it wasn't going to happen, because I wouldn't play along.''

"Yes.''

"And when Frank came clean, you realized you had a problem. You've got a complex plan to deal with, and nobody who understands it.''

"That's an oversimplification but, yes, that's the bottom line.''

"Well, Frank's a quick study.'' Megan smiled coldly. "It shouldn't take him more than, oh, two or three years to figure things out.''

"I'm sure you think that's amusing,'' Caz said, even more coldly, "but I'm returning to my country tomorrow. There's no time for Fisher to figure things out—even if he could, which I doubt.''

"And you want me to save your bacon.''

Caz ground his teeth together. Thank God she'd said it, because he doubted if he could.

"Yes.''

Megan smiled. "No.''

"What do you mean, no? Your company wrote this thing. We have a contract—''

"And you have Frank Fisher.'' She started past him, toward the door. "Good night, Sheikh Qasim. I wish I could say I'm sorry to see you sweat, but—''

Caz caught hold of her and spun her toward him. "All right,'' he said in a low voice, "that's it. I've had enough.''

"And so have I.'' Megan's voice trembled with suppressed anger. "If you think I'm going to go along with you and Simpson, that I'm going to sit by a phone here in Los Angeles and feed information to Frank Fisher—"

"Fisher is out of the picture," Caz snapped.

"Try telling that to Jerry Simpson!"

"I already did. That's how I got your address."

"And I'm telling you again, you've wasted your time. I will not let Frank use my work, my ideas, my—"

"Damn it, woman, will you shut up and let me talk? I'm offering you the job!"

That did it. For the first time since he'd met her, Megan O'Connell was speechless. She just stared at him, eyes wide with shock, hair loose in a froth of autumn-colored curls, face scrubbed free of makeup.

He remembered what he'd tried to forget. That kiss. The taste. The feel of her in his arms, of her lips parted to his...

"The job?"

Caz cleared his throat. "The job you were supposed to have, as my financial consultant. Will you accept?"

Would she accept? Her career had just done a 180, and the man was asking if she'd accept!

"You'd still be working for Tremont, Burnside and Macomb at your regular salary arrangement, but I'd add a bonus."

"Really," she said, hoping she sounded casual.

Caz named a figure. Megan decided it was a good thing he was still holding her arm or she might have fainted with shock.

"Is that satisfactory, Miss O'Connell?"

It was wild, not satisfactory, but she wasn't going to let him off that easy.

"You offered more when you thought you could buy me off."

He nodded. "Very well. One hundred thousand dollars. Will that do?"

"It will," she said, as if that much money fell into her lap every day.

"Good." He hesitated. "There's just one problem."

"What problem?"

"The status of women in the traditional culture of my country."

"You mean, their status in your eyes."

"That isn't what I said."

"You are Suliyam, your highness. You made that clear this morning. All you have to do is wave your scepter and change their status."

"It isn't that simple, damn it! I—"

He what? He was a master at international diplomacy, but how could he explain the culture of his forefathers to a fiery American redhead? She'd never understand it, even if he had the time, and he didn't. He was expected home tomorrow.

"If you expect me to help you, you're going to have to accept the fact that I'm a woman."

Accept it? Caz narrowed his eyes. He was painfully aware of it, even more so now that he was standing close to her, inhaling a faint lemony fragrance that reminded him of the orchards at Khaliar in midsummer.

"I can accept it," he said carefully. "However, despite your view of me, Miss O'Connell, I can't change centuries of tradition in my country overnight."

"Then how can you offer me a job?"

She wasn't going to like this, and he knew it. "There's only one solution. I'll openly acknowledge you as my consultant in-house, at Tremont, Burnside and Macomb. In financial circles in general, if you wish." He cleared his throat. "But we'll adhere to Simpson's plan. Fisher will fly to Suliyam with me, you'll stay here and—"

"No."

"I'll double your bonus."

"I said no."

"Miss O'Connell—"

Megan folded her arms and began tapping her foot. Not a good sign, Caz thought uneasily. He remembered that from the morning.

"You really have a problem with that word," she said coldly. "Must be a cultural thing. Here, in the States, 'en oh' means—"

"I know what it means," Caz said, trying hard to sound reasonable, "but these are special circumstances."

"You're right. You want me to help you perpetuate a lie."

"How much clearer can I be? I'll have to take the proposal to my people. I'll need Fisher beside me."

"What good would Frank do if he had to do his running-to-the-bathroom routine each time someone asked a question?"

It was an excellent point, one Caz had been doing his best to ignore.

"No good at all," Megan said without waiting for him to answer. "Your choice, your highness. Me, or nobody."

It wasn't a choice. Caz knew that. He'd known it ever since he'd unmasked Fisher.

"Well? Do I go to Suliyam or don't I?"

"You drive a hard bargain," Caz said coldly.

"Is that a yes?"

"Assuming it is, you'll have to put up with some things you won't like."

Megan wanted to pump her fist in the air. Instead she smiled politely.

"I put up with today, didn't I?"

"For example, you can't walk beside me in public."

She wanted to laugh. Not walk beside him? "No problem," she said, pleased at the sincerity in her tone.

"You can't talk to me when we're with others. You'll direct your comments to Hakim, who will then repeat them to me."

"I can manage that." Another lie, but once she was in Suliyam, he'd see how wrong he was to think a man could keep a woman living in the ancient past.

He hesitated. "And there's one last thing…"

Megan lifted her eyebrows. "Yes?"

"But this one is strictly my problem, not yours."

"Well, what is it?"

Caz moved quickly, as he'd done in the morning. She knew what was going to happen, knew it in the sudden race of her heart as he clasped her shoulders and lifted her to her toes.

"I'll have to find a way to keep my hands off you," he said thickly, and crushed her mouth beneath his.

CHAPTER FIVE

HER mouth was warm as the sun and sweet as the flowers that grew in the gardens of his palace.

And welcoming.

So welcoming.

Caz felt as if he were sinking into the kiss.

There was no pretence this time. He saw her eyes widen in shock but the instant his lips brushed hers, she sighed, leaned into him and opened her mouth to his.

She wanted him as badly as he wanted her.

There was no way to pretend, not when he was holding her so close to him that he could hardly tell where his body ended and hers began. She was clinging to him, her arms wound around his neck, her breasts lush against his chest, her thighs hot against his.

The room, the world, everything but the woman in his arms, spun away. Caz whispered her name, slid his hands into the glorious mass of autumn curls that was her hair. He tilted her head back, exposed the long line of her throat to his kisses.

She moaned as he nipped her flesh with his teeth, then soothed the tiny wound with his tongue, and when he sought her mouth again she moved against him, a shift of her hips so that her pelvis thrust against his straining erection.

Caz groaned, slid his knee between hers and cupped her bottom. She made a wild little sound that sent a fierce surge of pleasure coursing through his blood.

He could have her now, and reality be damned.

"Please," she whispered against his mouth, "please..."

He put his hands under her sweatshirt and finally felt her naked skin against his questing palms. Felt the velvet-softness of her breasts, the delicate pearling of her nipples. He danced the tips of his fingers across that sweetly ruched flesh and she moaned.

There was a roaring in his ears. Now, it said, now...

But it was only the incessant ringing of the telephone.

They sprang part and stared at each other, her eyes wide with astonishment, his breathing ragged, and then his cell phone rang again and he swore viciously as he tore it from his pocket and put it to his ear.

"What?" he barked.

It was Hakim, calling about the orders Caz had given for their departure the next morning.

The words meant nothing. All he could think about was what had just happened, what would have happened if not for this call. He'd have made love to a woman he hardly knew, barely trusted...

He could read the same shocked realization in her face. It was drained of color except for two bright spots of crimson high on her cheeks and the soft pink of her mouth, swollen from the passion of his kisses. He wanted to say something reassuring, but what could a man say to a woman he'd almost ravished?

He liked women, liked the pleasures of mutual seduction. The teasing conversation. The brush of hands. The glances that said more than words, all of it leading to an inevitable culmination.

What he'd just shared with this woman wasn't that at all. They'd come together without any of the niceties of seduction. All that had mattered was the swift, hot rush of passion, the primitive need to taste, touch, possess.

He saw Megan's throat constrict as she swallowed. Then she turned her back to him and wrapped her arms around herself.

Was she trembling?

Hakim was still talking, droning on and on about the minuscule details of tomorrow's agenda. Reports to review, memos to dictate, all the things Caz had asked to be reminded of before the flight home but right now, he didn't give a damn for any of it.

All he could think about was what had happened. What *would* happen, if he went through with his plan to take Megan with him. She was a distraction he couldn't afford…but even now, with the scent of her still in his nostrils, he managed to summon enough reason to know he couldn't afford to leave her behind, either. Not if his plans for his country were to succeed.

There was only one solution, he thought, and interrupted his aide in midsentence.

"A change of plans, Hakim. Mr. Fox won't be going with us tomorrow. You will send a car for Miss O'Connell, instead."

"You are taking the woman with you, Sheikh Qasim?"

The tone in Hakim's voice made Caz narrow his eyes. "I am."

"But a woman…"

"You will pick her up at seven."

"My lord. Surely you do not intend to—"

"Hakim. Surely *you* do not intend to question me." Caz spoke harshly. It was deliberate. No one questioned his orders. That was more than tradition; it was the law. It would change someday—it had to, if Suliyam were to flourish in these new times—but his aide's reaction to learning that Megan would return with them was only a small taste of what lay ahead. It had to be stopped, and quickly. "I gave you an order. You will obey it."

A beat of silence. A clearing of the throat. Then, at last, acquiescence. "Yes, my lord."

"There are things you will do before morning," Caz said, and enumerated them.

"I will see to everything."

"I'm sure you—"

"Tell him not to bother."

Caz turned around. Megan glared at him, eyes hot with anger. So much for his thinking that what had happened had left her shaken. He glared right back at her.

"Be quiet," he hissed.

"I heard you telling your flunky to round up the things you think I'll need for this trip, and—"

Caz caught her wrist. "Silence!"

"You cannot talk to me that way! I'm not one of your servants. I don't take orders from—"

His hand closed over her mouth. Megan gasped, struggled, sank her teeth into his flesh. Caz winced at the pain but kept his voice steady as he spoke a few last words to Hakim before snapping the cell phone shut.

Then he let go of Megan.

A mistake, he thought grimly, as she came at him with both hands balled into fists. He caught her wrists again and tugged her hands behind her back.

"You insufferable son of a bitch!"

"I was in the middle of a conversation," he said coldly. "When I am, you are not to interrupt."

"You were in the middle of snapping out orders," she said, her face livid with fury, "and I'll interrupt whenever I please!"

"Not me," he said through his teeth. "Do you understand?"

"What I understand is that your boy doesn't have to bother rounding up those things you told him to buy."

Caz raised his eyebrows. "You won't need a portable computer?"

"No more than I'll need the printer and fax, or the files from my office. I'm not going with you."

"You are."

"No, I'm not. I'd sooner go to the jungle with Tarzan than to a—a backward pile of sand with someone like you."

Caz took a quick step toward her. "You are not to speak that way about my country or me."

"I'll speak any damned way I like, and if you grab me again, so help me, I'll scream!"

She would. He believed her. That was all he needed. It was another tabloid headline in the making.

"Listen to me, Megan. If you treat me with disrespect, you'll ruin what I'm trying to do."

"What's that? To be even more loathsome than you already are?"

"And you'll endanger yourself. My people will not tolerate such behavior toward me from anyone, especially a woman."

"Then it's a good thing I'll never meet your people."

Caz gritted his teeth. "We reached an agreement. You're going with me to Suliyam."

"In a pig's eye!"

"A most inelegant expression."

"I know others you'll like even less."

"My car will come for you at seven," he said, refusing to be side-tracked.

Her smile was deadly sweet. "You car will stand at the curb and turn to rust before I set foot inside it."

"We have an agreement," he said grimly.

"You already said that. To hell with your agreement!

Why any woman would be fool enough to do anything you say—"

"Is that who you are now? A woman?"

Megan cocked her head and looked at him through narrowed eyes. "What's that supposed to mean?"

"I just like to know who I'm dealing with, that's all. You've just said a woman would be a fool to do anything I say."

"She would be."

"A while ago, you made the point that you weren't a woman at all."

"Don't be ridiculous! I never said—"

"You claim to be a professional. A person whose only identity lies in those initials after her name. B.A. M.B.A. C.P.A."

"You left out C.F.P.," Megan said coldly. "Certified Financial Planner. And if you're trying to make a point, I can't figure out what it is."

"My point is that you take refuge in the identity that suits you at a given moment."

"You make me sound schizophrenic!"

"Do I?" Caz folded his arms. "When I met you this morning, you made a case for being judged by your ability, not your gender."

"Something you're incapable of, apparently."

"Are you suggesting what happened just now wasn't mutual?"

She felt herself turn color, but she kept her eyes on his. "I'm not going with you, Sheikh Qasim. That's final."

"You're making something out of nothing. What happened was a mistake."

"It certainly was. And it could never, ever, not in a million years, happen again."

"Another point of agreement. Which is why you're going with me tomorrow."

"I'd sooner—"

"Swing through the trees with Tarzan. Yes, I know, but then, you don't have a contract with Tarzan."

"I don't have one with you, either," Megan said, but even in her anger, she knew what he was getting at.

"You do. A verbal contract, enforceable in any court of law." He fleshed that I-Am-Brilliant smile that made her fingers itch to slap it from his face. "I'm sure you're aware of that, Miss O'Connell, considering your familiarity with what constitutes grounds for a lawsuit."

"You wouldn't sue." Megan flashed a smile that she hoped was the equal of his. "You wouldn't want the publicity."

"There's a difference between negative publicity and positive publicity. I'd get lots of excellent mileage out of my heartfelt attempts to hire a woman, only to find that woman unwilling to take on the responsibility of a difficult assignment."

"Your people wouldn't like to hear that you'd tried to hire a woman."

"My people will believe what I tell them, and I'll tell them that the press lies."

"I'd phone every newspaper, tell them what actually happened…"

"In that case, so would I. I don't think it would add much to your professional image if I described what went on in this room in intimate detail, do you?"

He smiled again. God, she hated that smile! It was so smug. How easily she could slap it from his face…but that wouldn't change the fact that he was right.

"I really, really despise you, Sheikh Qasim."

"A pity, Miss O'Connell. I was hoping you'd want to

head up my fan club." The tight smile vanished from his lips. "Your boss has me backed into a corner, Megan. Like it or not, this job is yours by default."

She glared at him. He glared back. He had her trapped, and he knew it.

"How long is this assignment going to last?"

Caz considered telling her the truth, then decided against it. She wouldn't want to hear that she might be expelled from Suliyam in a day, if things went badly, or that she might still be there months from now, if things went well.

"I don't know." That was the truth, more or less.

"A week."

He shrugged his shoulders, as if he were considering the possibility.

"Two weeks is the longest I'll stay. Agreed?"

"Absolutely. Two weeks is the longest you wish to stay." That was the truth, too. Whose fault was it if she misinterpreted his answer? At least she wasn't fighting him anymore.

"Must I fly out tomorrow? That doesn't give me much time."

"For what?" Caz felt a knot form in his belly. "If you think I'm going to delay my plans so you can say goodbye to a lover—"

"I have a family," Megan said coolly. "I want to let them know where I'm going."

"You can phone them from my plane," he said, and tried not to acknowledge the sense of relief he felt. Not that he cared about her personal life. She could have a dozen lovers, if she liked, so long as such commitments didn't impinge on her work for him.

"I suppose it would be foolish for me to think your Hakim can't buy computers and move files in the middle of the night."

"You're right. It would be." Caz's smile was saccharine sweet. "There are some benefits to being a king." He shot back his cuff and checked his watch. "Any other questions?"

Megan almost laughed. She had more questions than she could count, beginning with why she'd ever wanted this assignment, but it was too late to ask them now.

"No, thank you," she said politely. "Not at the moment."

"One last thing. About the kinds of clothing you'll need to pack…"

"I'm a big girl, Sheikh Qasim. I don't need you to tell me what to do."

Caz had to admire her. She was beautiful, stubborn, defiant…and most definitely unimpressed by his titles or his wealth.

No wonder he found her desirable.

She was completely different from any of the women he'd been involved with. His lovers were invariably beautiful, invariably bright—despite what this American clearly thought of him, he'd always found unintelligent women dull.

But no woman ever disagreed with him, much less spoke to him with such boldness. No matter their nationality, they were always eager to please.

Not Megan O'Connell.

And, of course, that was the reason for the attraction. Knowing it didn't change things, but it would definitely make it easier to resist. Caz felt a weight lift from his shoulders.

"I was only going to point out that the desert can be as cool at night as it is hot during the day," he said pleasantly, "but let's not quarrel over it." He held out his hand. She looked at it for a long moment, then put her palm against his. Heat, almost enough to burn his palm, seemed to flash from that innocent contact point straight to his groin. He was sure she felt something, too, if only because of her quick intake of breath, but he forced a smile to his lips. "To a successful collaboration, Miss O'Connell."

"To one that ends quickly, Sheikh Qasim."

Her expression was defiant. He thought about pulling her into his arms again and changing that insolent look to a look of passion, but sanity prevailed.

"Good night, Megan."

"Good night, Qasim."

His brows lifted but he didn't say anything. Still, as he stepped into the damp night, he laughed softly to himself. She was, as the Americans would say, some piece of work. Calling him by his given name. No honorific, no title... It was, he supposed, her way of making sure he knew she wasn't impressed.

Caz turned up his collar, slipped behind the wheel of his Lamborghini and turned the ignition key.

These next weeks would be interesting, but they wouldn't last forever. Someday, they would meet on different terms, he as a man, she as a woman. When they did, he'd put an end to all this nonsense. He'd take her to bed and keep her there until she begged for mercy, until the both of them sated their hunger and grew weary of each other.

He pulled away from the curb, his headlights boring into the darkness of the California night.

Someday, he'd have all of Megan O'Connell he wanted.

But not yet.

CHAPTER SIX

Wнат did you pack for a trip to a place that was still a mystery to the world?

Megan phoned Briana. Her sister wasn't in, so she left a message on her voice mail.

Hi, Bree. I'm leaving for a place called Suliyam tomorrow early in the A.M. Details when I get back but boy, I wish you were there. Maybe you could help me figure out what to pack. Anyway, hope you're having fun. Talk to you in a week or two.

Sighing, she headed for the bedroom, flung open the door to the closet and stared inside. Bree had more stamps and visas on her passport than any of them except, maybe, Sean. But the odds were that not even Bree could have advise her on what was right for this trip.

Maybe she should have listened to Qasim when he'd tried to give her advice, but she'd been so furious with him by then that listening to anything he had to say was beyond her.

Don't cut off your nose to spite your face, her mother would have warned, just as she had years ago when Megan was fourteen and moaning over the fact that nobody had asked her to a school dance. Fallon, a stunner at sixteen with boys tripping over each other in efforts to please her, had volunteered one of them as an escort.

"Tommy says he'd love to take you, Meg," she'd said.

"He just wants to score points with you."

"Maybe," Fallon had said cheerfully. "But he's cute, he's nice, and you'll have fun."

"No, I won't. Tell him to forget about it."

Megan spent the night of the dance at home, looking sad and hoping for pity from her mother. Instead Mary had told her to stop sulking, followed by that no-nonsense advice about the folly of refusing something you really wanted, just to make a point.

Megan sighed and sank down on the edge of her bed.

Good counsel then. Great counsel now. Too bad she hadn't been ready to admit it an hour ago.

She knew a bit about Suliyam's culture, a lot about its finances and natural resources, thanks to her research, but that was it. What was the weather like, this time of year? What was its capital city like, and was that where they were going? What sort of hotel would she be in?

And what about that comment Qasim had made, that she wouldn't be able to speak to him when they met with his people? He'd sounded dead serious. Not that it mattered. She'd change that first thing. There'd been no sense in saying so because it would just have led to a quarrel and that was all they'd done since they met.

Well, no. They'd done more than that. They'd turned each other on with a touch.

That last kiss had been enough to turn her inside out. It didn't make sense. Qasim wasn't her type.

Megan rolled her eyes.

That was the understatement of the century. He was a king. A sheikh. A man tied to a past she could hardly imagine. Of course, he wasn't he wasn't her type.

Was that why they were so drawn to each other? Was it the old "opposites attract" thing? He was undoubtedly accustomed to women who didn't think for themselves; she dated men who treated women as equals. She'd never met a man who went through life taking what he wanted until today.

His attitude was infuriating. It was irritating.

It was incredibly exciting.

Soon, she'd be alone with him in a foreign land with none of the intrusions of the world to keep them from what they both wanted and yes, it was what she wanted, too. Qasim in her bed, his hands on her, his mouth…

Megan shot to her feet.

They wouldn't be alone, they'd be working. An employer and his employee. Better still, a financial advisor and her client. There'd be no time for the male-female thing. Why was she sitting around thinking about nonsense? She had to pack, and why was she giving a moment's thought to *what* to pack?

For all she knew, woman in Qasim's country wore potato sacks. So what? She wore suits, sensible heels, and panty hose. Why on earth would she change that? Why would she change anything about herself for this job or this man?

Megan took her suitcase from the shelf and began tossing garments into it.

She knew who she was.

Soon, so would the sheikh.

Three days later, sitting in her rooms in Qasim's palace, she wondered at the innocence of that assessment.

Who was she? A woman in a harem, that was who. All right. Not a harem. She was in the women's quarters, but it came to the same thing.

It turned out there was no hotel in Suliyam's capital city. Qasim had explained that as they'd been whisked from the airport to his palace.

She had to admit the palace was magnificent, gleaming under the hot sun like something out of a fairy tale. Her rooms were handsome: large, airy and elegant, with tiled floors and Moorish windows, and the view of a tranquil pond in a beautiful courtyard garden was to die for.

It was all perfect, except for the fact that she'd been relegated to the women's quarters.

"The what?" she'd said the first day, her voice rising in disbelief as Qasim led her along a series of corridors to a set of enormous double doors.

"The women's quarters, and keep your voice down. It's bad enough I'm permitting you to walk beside me where others can see us."

The arrogance of the remark had put a slow burn in her belly. And what "others" was he talking about? The bowing minions who'd greeted them on the front steps? The stony-faced guards who looked like leftovers from a bad late-night movie?

Megan had stopped in her tracks. "I don't give a damn about others, and I am not going to be relegated to purgatory just so you can maintain the status quo."

"You understood the rules when you came here."

"So did you. I'm your financial consultant, not a member of your harem."

He'd given a long-suffering sigh, as if her irritation were nothing more than he'd expected.

"I'm simply ensuring my people show you the necessary respect."

"And that means I have to live like Scheherazade? Next thing you'll tell me is that I'm going to have a eunuch around to make sure I behave!"

"Sorry," he'd said, so straight-faced that she'd almost believed him, "I fired the last eunuch a couple of months ago." His hand had closed on her elbow. "My grandfather was the last to keep a harem. Now, stop arguing and keep walking."

"You can't give me orders!"

His hand had tightened on her arm. "Use that tone to me again," he'd said in a low voice, "and you'll learn what purgatory really is."

"I already know. It's being here, with you."

"Is that supposed to upset me, Megan? It doesn't. I don't give a damn what you think of me or this place, just as long as you do your job." He'd opened the doors to the rooms that were now hers; a covey of giggling women had rushed forward to surround her. "Your servants," Qasim had said dryly, as if he knew being presented with servants would only add to her bad temper. While the ladies in question oohed and ahhed and touched her blue wool suit with exploratory hands, he'd bent forward and put his mouth to her ear so only she could hear him. "You want to know the truth, *kalila?* I think what angers you is that you know you'll be far away from me."

When pigs fly, she'd have told him, but the women had started trying to strip off her jacket and while she was fending them off, Qasim shut the doors and left her.

Now it was what she'd come to think of as Day Three of her Incarceration. She'd come all this distance to do her job, but she hadn't done a damned thing except pace her rooms and the garden outside.

And she'd had enough.

Megan shot to her feet, went out to the garden, opened the gate and marched down to the sea. The women rushed after her, crying out in distress. Apparently she wasn't supposed to leave her cage.

She ignored them.

At least she could breathe down here. Why had she tolerated such treatment? To come all this way only to be treated like a prisoner?

A sea bird called out overhead, but its cry offered no answers.

The situation was intolerable.

"Intolerable," Megan snapped.

She turned on her heel and retraced her steps back to the garden, to her rooms, to the double doors that she yanked open so she could march past the astonished guards while her women danced around her wringing their hands and wailing...

And stopped dead when she saw, just ahead, the Great Hall she remembered from the night of their arrival.

The Great Hall, and Qasim.

Qasim, and a woman.

A beautiful woman, even at a distance, petite and delicate with midnight-black hair that fell to her waist. Her gown was pale peach, so delicate it might have been spun from sunlight. She stood close to Qasim, bodies almost touching, her hands on his shoulders, her face turned up to his.

He's going to kiss her, Megan thought.

For the first time in her life, she understood what people meant when they said anguish could feel like a knife wound to the heart.

She must have made a sound because Qasim turned and saw her. She waited, unmoving. He would say something. Do something. Acknowledge her presence, come to her and explain that what she saw—what she thought she saw—was nothing.

Instead, he turned back to the woman, brought her hands to his mouth, put his arm around her waist and led her up a wide staircase. Led her to his bed. Where else would a man take a woman who looked at him with stars in her eyes?

Megan's servants surrounded her, scolding and tut-tutting and tugging at her hands. She let them lead her back to her rooms but when the doors closed behind her, she tore free of them, cursing Qasim and her own stupidity for being upset over something that should never have upset her, ranting in words that probably would have surprised her brothers.

The women watched her, wide-eyed, whispering among themselves and keeping their distance which, for some stupid reason, only increased her fury. Finally she snatched up a small porcelain vase and hurled it at the wall.

That got her audience moving.

"La, la," one said while another wagged her finger. It didn't take a genius to figure out that meant "no," but "no" wasn't going to work.

Qasim had ignored her here for three endless days, all so he could play games with another woman.

Enough. She'd come here to do a job. If she wasn't going to do it, she was going to go home.

Megan stormed to the doors and yanked them open. The guards looked at her as if she were the last person on earth they ever wanted to see again.

"I want to see the king. Damn it, don't look at me as if you're both deaf. Surely one of you understands what I'm saying. I want to see your precious sheikh. Qasim. Do you hear me? You are to take me to—"

"Good afternoon, Miss O'Connell."

The guards snapped to attention, then parted to reveal Hakim. Her serving women gasped and fell to the floor around her, doubled over like plump, silk-swathed hassocks.

"Stand up," Megan snapped, "you shouldn't kneel to any man!"

The women didn't move. They had no idea what she was saying but Hakim did. His eyes were cold as he clapped his hands and barked out a command that sent the women scuttling away.

"It is unwise to interfere in matters you don't comprehend, Miss O'Connell."

"Take me to your king."

"That is why I've come. His highness wishes to see you."

"It's a damned good thing he does."

"My lord does not like his women to use rough language."

"Then it's a good thing I'm not his woman. Where is he?"

"He waits for me to bring you to him."

God, the man was insufferable! Almost as arrogant as Qasim but then, Qasim probably wouldn't employ him otherwise. They started toward the Great Hall. Halfway there, Megan swept past the aide. Walking behind him, even if he were leading her somewhere, infuriated her.

She could hardly wait to confront Qasim. She'd tell the mighty Pooh-Bah what she thought of him, his harem, his servants and his country. Then she'd give him a choice. Put her to work or send her home. She'd be damned if she'd spend another day feeling useless while he did who knew what...

While he took a woman with long black hair to his bed.

They reached the Great Hall. Megan started toward the stairs. Hakim stepped in front of her.

"My lord waits for you outside."

"Your lord," Megan mimicked coldly.

Hakim's eyes flashed as she brushed past him. The guards at the huge entrance doors flung the doors wide. Megan stepped out into the sunlight, clattered down the steps...and stopped.

A Humvee stood in the curved driveway, engine purring, rear door open. Qasim stood next to it, Qasim dressed in white linen trousers and a white linen shirt with the sleeves rolled back, so beautiful, so desert-fierce with the sun beating down on his dark head that she felt her bones turn liquid.

A smile curved his lips as she started down the steps, and she remembered how those lips had felt against hers, how the hand he held out had felt against her breast the last time they'd been together.

"Megan," he said, and the truth shot through her quicksilver, the realization that part of her anger, all of it, lay in knowing that he hadn't come to her, come for her, and in knowing now that it was because he had someone else.

How could she have hidden that truth from herself? How could she want a man like him?

Her heart turned to stone. She'd never been a fool for a man and she'd be damned if she'd start now.

She took a breath, let it out and took another. Then, smiling, she went down the steps. When she reached him, she put her hand in his. He started to raise it to his lips but she remembered that scene a little while ago, the woman a breath from him, her hands against his mouth, and she pulled her hand down and gave him a vigorous handshake.

"Sheikh Qasim," she said politely. "It's good to see you. I'd started to think you'd changed your mind about working with me."

One dark eyebrow rose in a questioning arch. "Certainly not. In fact…" He motioned to the open door of the Hummer. "We're on our way to our first meeting this morning."

"I'm glad to hear it, but you might have done me the courtesy of telling me so in advance."

"My apologies," he said, climbing into the Hummer after her. He closed the door, tapped lightly on a glass partition that separated them from the driver and the vehicle shifted gears and started forward. "I've been busy."

"Yes. So I noticed."

He looked at her. "Sorry?"

"Nothing." She looked down at her skirt and smoothed it over her knees. "I want to talk about the rooms you've given me."

"Aren't they to your liking?"

"No, they're not. They're very handsome, but I resent being kept prisoner."

He'd looked uneasy a minute ago. Now, he sat back and laughed.

"The women's quarters are hardly a prison."

"They are to me. I came here to work. Instead I've spent my time doing nothing in an isolated part of the palace."

"I'm sorry about that, too. Some things came up that had to be dealt with."

"Yes. So I noticed."

She wanted to bite off her tongue, but it was too late.

"Am I missing something here, Megan?"

"Only that I'd like to get busy on our project."

"Of course. And since today seems to be my day for apologies, let me make one more. I should have explained why I put you in the women's quarters. It was for your own sake. I wanted to be sure my people understand our relationship. You're unmarried, you see, and a foreigner."

"And?"

"And, it's important we avoid any hint of impropriety."

"Ah. Then I take it that the woman I saw you with a little while ago is married as well as Suliyamese, or that you don't give a damn about any hints of impropriety where she's concerned."

Qasim looked surprised. Dear God, so was she! Had she really said something so stupid? His eyes darkened; they locked on hers and she felt a flood of heat rise in her face.

"I'm only asking as a matter of curiosity," she said stiffly. "You keep telling me about all these customs and traditions…"

"Alayna is one of us, yes."

One of us. Who was he kidding? The lady was more than that.

"But she isn't married."

"I see. In other words, it's all right for you to be seen with an unmarried woman as long as that woman isn't me?"

Qasim looked at her for an endless few seconds. Then he gave her a slow, sexy grin. "Are you jealous, *kalila?*"

"Certainly not. I told you, I'm just—"

"Curious." He sighed, as if a weight were on his shoulders, and his smile faded. "Alayna is my cousin."

His cousin. That gorgeous creature was his cousin. Why did she feel such a sense of relief? Qasim could have a dozen beautiful women around him, for all she cared.

"I would have introduced you, but Alayna has some personal problems just now. That was why she came to see me. To discuss them."

"You don't have to explain."

Qasim reached for her hand. She let him take it—it would have been ridiculous to try and tug it back—and tried to pretend she didn't feel the rush of heat his touch sent racing along her skin.

"I should not have neglected you these past days, Megan. It's just that I had many things to attend to."

Things like assuring Alayna that he would find a way to keep her from having to marry a man who had been chosen for her, that she could, instead, marry a man she loved. That, alone, had involved him for two days. And, after that, the careful plans he'd made for the first meeting he and Megan would attend had started coming apart.

It would be the most difficult of the meetings because it involved Ahmet, one of the most powerful traditionalists in Suliyam. Caz had arranged to meet with Ahmet and his men here, in the palace, to make no mention of Megan's presence beforehand.

But Ahmet had phoned yesterday to say he'd fallen ill and couldn't travel. Would Qasim bring the meeting to him, at his ancestral home deep in the mountains beyond the vast desert that stretched away from the sea?

"It would be a generous thing to do, my lord," Ahmet had said in a wheezing voice.

The wheeze struck Caz as overdone. He suspected the suggestion had less to do with illness and more to do with a power play, but going to Ahmet instead of demanding the man come to him was a gesture of respect that could help his cause.

The change in venue meant he'd had to tell Ahmet he was bringing a woman with him.

Ahmet had responded with outrage and disbelief. "How could such a thing be?" he'd said.

Caz had lied through his teeth. The woman was a clerk, he told him, sent by the company she worked for to keep their records organized. It was, he added, customary for western firms to employ females in positions too unimportant to be filled by men.

"Ah." Ahmet had chuckled. "Now I see. She is a meaningless creature."

"Absolutely," Qasim had answered, though he'd wanted to laugh. Megan O'Connell, meaningless? Wouldn't she love to hear that? She wouldn't; he wasn't stupid.

As for the traditions she'd encounter on this journey... Caz looked at her now, sitting beside him in the Hummer, dressed in that ridiculous wool suit and sensible pumps, and almost groaned.

If she thought the arrangements at his palace were restrictive, he could only guess at how she'd react to life in the territory ruled by Ahmet.

He felt a vague sense of unease, taking her on this trip, but if she behaved herself, things would go well. And he'd see to it she behaved herself, like it or not.

He wasn't looking forward to dealing with what came next. He'd always thought of himself as fearless. After all, death came to every man eventually. Why quake when a lion decides you look like dinner, which had happened to him on a photographic safari in South Africa? Why run when an assassin came at you out of the dark, as one had in the uncertain days after his father's death?

The trouble was, dealing with lions and assassins was easier than dealing with the temper of the woman beside him. So far, the only way he'd found to deal with her anger was to take her in his arms, and that was proving more dangerous than anything he'd ever done before.

"Are you going to tell me where we're going, or is it another of your deep, dark secrets?"

She had a half smile on her lips. Apparently she'd decided to forgive him. Too bad the smile wasn't going to last.

"We're driving to my helicopter."

"Your what?"

She was still smiling, but she was also looking at him as if he'd lost his mind. Maybe he had.

"It would take days to make the trip by land. It's only a couple of hours by air." He hesitated. "Megan. This place we're going to... You'll have to make some accommodations."

She gave a little sigh, but she wasn't angry. Not yet. "What now? Won't walking behind you be enough?"

"We're flying into an ancient city. Tradition—"

"Don't tell me." She flashed that smile again. "If you expect me to fold myself in half and bow—"

"That might not be a bad idea," he said. She shot him a look that made him laugh. "I'm joking. But..." His gaze drifted over her, then returned to her face. "You can't enter Ahmet's lands dressed like that."

The smile flickered. "Ahmet's a fashion maven?"

"You must wear what he thinks is appropriate for a woman as a sign of respect."

The smile died. Caz sighed; trouble lay directly ahead.

"And what would you like me to wear, Sheikh Qasim? Sackcloth and ashes?"

"The women of his village dress traditionally."

"There's that word again."

"Caftans, slit at the ankles," Caz said, refusing to be drawn into a battle. "Sandals."

"Shackles, too?"

"Did you never hear the saying, 'When in Rome...'"

"Roman women had more status than they do here."

"That's changing."

Megan folded her arms. "Not that I can see!"

A muscle knotted in Caz's jaw. "Must you fight me over everything?" His voice hardened. "You insisted you were the right person for this job. Are you?"

She swung toward him, ready to take him on, but the look on his face stopped her. Besides, he was right. Why wave a red flag in front of a bull? It just made her uneasy to give up her western suit for a caftan, and wasn't that silly? She'd still be the same woman...

She would, wouldn't she?

"Megan?"

Reluctantly she nodded. "Yes. All right. If I have to—"

"Good. I've told my driver to stop just before we reach the helipad. He'll set up a small tent. You can use it as a dressing room." Caz hesitated. "There's one other thing."

"Now what?"

"I've explained that you're a clerk."

Her eyes widened. She looked, he thought, as if he'd slapped her.

"Are you crazy? I am not going to let you pass me off as—"

She gasped as he reached out and caught her by the shoulders.

"What do you want them to think, damn it? In their world, there's only one reason a man would take a woman with him on such a trip."

"I have three degrees," she said, knowing how foolish she sounded, knowing, too, that she could not, would not let him relegate her to the role he'd clearly intended for her all along. "I will not—"

"You will do as you're told. Or—"

"Stop threatening me! You won't send me back home. You can't." Her eyes were bright with challenge. "You need me, Qasim, and you know it."

"You're right," he said through clenched teeth. "I need you here, but there's another solution." Heat slammed through his blood as he pulled her into his arms. "I'll simply let them think you belong to me."

His mouth claimed hers. She struggled, but only for the time it took him to nip her bottom lip and slide his tongue into her mouth. Then she made a little sound of surrender and arched against him, returning his kisses, crying out when he put his hand under her jacket, cupped her breast, felt the nipple rise and thrust against his palm.

He let her go so abruptly that she fell back in the seat. He had to; otherwise, he knew he'd have pushed up her skirt, freed himself, taken her, taken her, taken her…

She stared at him, her eyes bright with angry tears.

"I despise you," she whispered, and Caz decided that made a lot of sense because right now, he despised himself, too.

CHAPTER SEVEN

THE helicopter flew over a land that was as untamed as it was beautiful.

Undulating waves of golden sand. Vivid patches of dark green, guarding sapphire-blue pools of water. A vulture with black-tipped wings, soaring in lazy circles and once, most startling of all, a herd of horses galloped under the dark shadow of the 'copter as it passed over them.

Megan had questions about the land, the animals that lived on it, the village they were flying to, but there was no one to ask. Qasim sat across from her in icy removal, reading papers he'd taken from his briefcase as soon as they'd boarded.

She was on her own.

Well, that was fine with her. She had her own notes to read through, and any questions she had about where they were going would be answered soon enough. For a little while, she lost herself in facts and figures, but they began to blur and, finally, she closed her notebook and put it away.

She couldn't concentrate. She was nervous, though she'd sooner have died than admit it.

What would it be like, this place where the customs of an earlier time prevailed? Where she'd have to pretend to be a docile creature with no opinions or thoughts of her own?

She'd been assigned a role. Like it or not she was already playing it. She looked down at the dress she now wore.

Qasim hadn't mentioned it would be spun of cotton so fine it felt like silk or that it would have tiny pale blue flowers embroidered along the cuffs and hem. The skirt was slit to the knee on each side; the neckline was a sort of modified cowl, so that it could be drawn up as a hood against the chill that settled in the mountains at night.

Megan wiggled her feet, bare in the soft-as-butter thong sandals. You couldn't very well wear stockings with a strip of leather between your toes.

Standing in the little tent Qasim's driver had erected, wearing these new things, she'd felt a funny hollowness in the pit of her stomach. She'd looked back at the little pile of clothing she'd discarded, her suit and blouse, her panty hose and shoes.

Was this how a wild creature felt when it left the safety of its old skin behind?

What would Qasim think, when he saw her?

That she looked like an obedient female, she'd thought, and that had been enough to make her stop thinking like a silly girl and think like the woman she was.

"Am I suitably dressed, oh Lord of the World?" she'd said coolly, stepping out of the tent.

Qasim's gaze had darkened and moved slowly over her.

"You'll do," he'd finally replied, and there'd been a huskiness in his voice that had made her want to go to him, frame his face with her hands, bring his mouth to hers and ask him what he really thought, if he liked the way the thin cotton clung to her breasts, to her hips...

Megan picked up her notes and went back to work.

Ahmet's mountain village wasn't a village at all.

It was a medieval fortress.

Stepping out of the helicopter, staring at the horsemen who'd come racing out the gates brandishing steel-tipped lances, Megan shivered as the men let out a bloodcurdling roar.

Qasim caught hold of her hand. She didn't even think of trying to pull away. Instead, she laced her fingers through his and moved closer, until she was almost leaning against him.

"They're honoring me," he whispered. "Don't be afraid."

The horsemen stopped a hundred yards away. Silver bells adorned their horses' bridles and played softly as the animals tossed their heads. The riders gave an eerie, ululating cry and spurred their mounts into a gallop. Qasim gave her hand one last squeeze. Then he stepped away from her, laughing as the riders surrounded him in a river of horses and spears. A man rode forward, leading a stallion with a coat like black silk. Qasim grabbed the horse's flowing mane and leaped into the saddle.

Another wild cry, and the horsemen galloped toward the gates of the city.

The wind tossed Megan's hair over her eyes. Her hand shook as she brushed it back; she could feel her heart racing. She felt as if she'd been sucked up by a tornado and tossed back through time. She wanted to turn and run, but where would she go without Qasim?

She saw a small group of women coming toward her, materializing like ghosts from the blowing dust left by the horses. Their faces were stern and set in lines of distrust as they gathered around her. One, perhaps the eldest, reached out, fingered Megan's auburn hair and said something that made the rest laugh.

It was the kind of laugh that sent a chill down Megan's spine. She jerked her head away, took a deep breath and fixed the woman with a steady look.

"My name is Megan," she said, "and I am with Sheikh Qasim."

Those words, she sensed, would be her only protection.

Two days later, Megan felt as if she were going crazy.

She hated this place, hated everyone who lived in it, hated Qasim for bringing her to it...

Hated herself, for having let him lead her into a nightmare.

She spent her days at meetings, playing the part of an obedient slave, and spent her nights in this room, pacing like a caged animal. The room was enormous, easily the size of her entire apartment back home. The walls were tiled, the floors carpeted. She supposed you could describe her surroundings as beautiful.

But it was still a cage.

Compared to this, the harem in Qasim's palace had been heaven with its little garden, its reflecting pool, the soft breeze that blew in from the sea.

Here, she had only the four walls that enclosed her. At day's end, Hakim walked her to the door and left her to the ministrations of a pair of sullen women who brought her evening meal—a glob of unidentifiable something on a chipped plate that looked as if it had never been washed, a pitcher of liquid that tasted like warm beer, and a hunk of flat, tasteless bread. The women never responded to Megan's attempts at communication.

Hakim wasn't much better. When she complained at her treatment, he assured her that his master understood her situation, but when she demanded to see Qasim, he looked horrified and told her such a thing was out of the question.

Was Hakim telling her the truth? Did Qasim know what was happening? She had no idea. He acted as if she were invisible.

When she entered the meeting room the first day, just seeing him lifted her spirits.

"Qasim," she'd said softly, but he'd looked right through her. He'd warned her, told her what would be expected, but surely he could at least make eye contact? Didn't he want to know how she was being treated?

Hakim had pointed to a low stool behind his master. Megan had bristled. Sitting behind Qasim was one thing; sitting four inches off the floor with her knees tucked under her chin was another.

But the room had begun filling with men; she'd felt all those dark eyes on her and suddenly the stool behind Qasim had seemed like an eminently fine idea. She'd settled on it, struggled to find a way to get her long legs under her and her briefcase in her lap while she told herself the meeting and their time in this horrible place would not last more than a day.

Wrong.

It was two days later and they were still here.

Some things, at least, had changed for the better.

Qasim still ignored her. But the women who waited on her had taken to offering occasional smiles. She'd demanded Hakim arrange for her to get some air and last night, the women had produced lanterns and taken her for an hour's walk along cobblestone streets that twisted and turned and ended, abruptly, at the city wall.

Some of the changes were for the worse.

Ahmet had taken to looking at her. None of the other men did, not after that first time. They treated her as Qasim did, as if she were invisible.

Not Ahmet.

Qasim had said Ahmet was too ill to travel, but he didn't appear ill to Megan. He looked—there was no other word for it—evil. Evil, and fat, and filthy. And yes, he was always sneaking glances at her. She caught him a couple of times but mostly, she sensed him watching her. His eyes were like tiny black beetles. She could almost feel them crawling over her skin.

Like right now.

Megan shuddered. Concentrate on what you're doing, she told herself. Forget Ahmet, forget everything but the numbers and words on the papers in her lap, and Qasim's questions.

What a ridiculous procedure this was.

Qasim would address his comments to Hakim in his own tongue and then in English, probably so she'd have more time to find the information. Then she had to look at Hakim, give her answer to him so he could repeat it to Qasim.

It was a waste of time, and all done for no purpose she could see. Qasim had been worried her presence would offend the super-macho males of his country but how could she offend them when they ignored her?

Ignored her, except for Ahmet.

He was watching her again. She could feel it. She looked up and stared straight at him, something she knew was forbidden, but enough was enough.

Megan narrowed her eyes and gave him her best Don't-Mess-With-Me glare. It always worked with idiots who thought a woman alone in a restaurant was just aching to be hit on…but it didn't work now. Ahmet's beady little eyes assessed her with even greater interest. His tongue came out and licked slowly over his fleshy lips.

Her heart did a terrified two-step. She dragged her gaze from his and looked down, blindly, at the papers in her lap.

So much for staring him down. And so much for handling this on her own. Qasim might not want to talk to her, but she sure as hell wanted to talk to—

"Ouch!"

Megan swung around. Had someone kicked her? She rubbed her hip and glared at the man nearest to her. He glared back, spat a couple of guttural words and answered the question by kicking her again. It wasn't much of a kick, it was more a prod with the tip of his booted foot, but it was the final straw.

"What the hell do you think you're doing?" she said as she shot to her feet.

The room, normally humming with conversation, became completely silent. All eyes were on her now, even Qasim's.

"Sit down," he said quietly.

"I will not sit down! This—this pig just kicked me."

Qasim's eyes darkened. "I will deal with him later. For now, you must sit down."

"This is a horrible place." Megan's voice trembled as her anger gave way to the fear it disguised. "I want to leave. I want—"

"Sit!" Qasim roared.

She sank down on the stool, shaken and shaking. She sensed him glaring at her. Then he said something and everyone laughed.

She'd had never felt so alone in her life.

After a moment, Qasim cleared his throat. She heard the rustle of papers, the drone of his voice as the meeting continued, but she wasn't listening. Why had she ever agreed to his demands? He'd turned her into a woman she didn't know, brought her to a place where civilization didn't exist, abandoned her to the less-than-tender mercies of a gang of cutthroats...

"Miss O'Connell!"

She looked up. Hakim's face was like stone.

"My lord the Sheikh asked a question."

"I didn't... What question?"

"I will ask him to repeat it."

"Just tell me what it was."

"There is a procedure to follow," Hakim said coldly. "You will follow it."

He turned away from her to start the entire roundabout process again. Now she was supposed to sit patiently while Hakim posed a question to Qasim, wait again while Qasim replied in English, then in his own tongue. After that, she'd sit here docilely while Hakim repeated words she already understood. Then, only then, would she be permitted to speak.

To hell with that.

The English words were hardly out of Qasim's mouth when she replied to them.

For a second time, an awful silence filled the room. The men gave her startled, condemning glances.

Ahmet looked straight at her.

Megan had never had a man look at her that way, but the meaning was clear as glass. It sent a chill straight to the marrow of her bones.

She dragged her eyes from his and struggled to stay calm. All right. She'd made a mistake. Two of them, in one morning. She'd be more cautious from now on. When in Rome, Qasim had said, and he was right. Surely she could manage that for another couple of—

A hand closed on her wrist. She looked up, straight into Ahmet's ugly face. He grinned, revealing rotting teeth and revolting breath.

"*May-gahn.*"

"Yes?" she said politely, and tried not to inhale.

Ahmet jerked her to her feet. "You come."

"No. No, thank you, Mr. Ahmet, but—"

"You come now."

"Really, I don't think—"

Qasim stood up. His lips drew back from his teeth in the

semblance of a smile and he said something to Ahmet. Ahmet smiled, too, even more coldly. His hand tightened around her wrist.

"Megan," Qasim said softly, his eyes locked to the other man's face, "don't do or say anything."

"But—"

"Damn it, woman, listen to me! Say nothing. Do nothing. Do you understand?"

"Yes, but—"

Ahmet curved his arm around her. His hand lay at her waist. He chuckled, his stinking breath hot against her face, his fingers kneading her flesh. Qasim said something, his tone harsh and commanding. Ahmet replied to it, and Qasim spoke again. Ahmet laughed. His fingers were still moving. Up. Up. Up...

Megan growled, spun toward him and plowed her fist into his gut.

The room exploded with action.

Wild cries. The clatter of overturned chairs. Shouts and yells, and hands clawing for her dress, her hair...

Qasim swept her into his arms.

"Qasim," Megan sobbed, "oh, Qasim..."

"Be quiet," he snarled, "or I'll have what's left of your body fed to the jackals!"

Then he tossed her over his shoulder, shouldered his way through the mob and strode out the door.

Hours went by.

Perhaps only minutes.

Megan only knew she was hoarse from saying she was sorry. Still, as Qasim paced by her again, she said it once more.

"I'm sorry, Qasim. I didn't mean—"

"Be quiet!"

She nodded and sank down on the edge of a chair. Whatever she'd started in the meeting room wasn't good. She could hear voices raised in anger outside the door to her room—a door Qasim had bolted. The women who served her sat huddled in a corner, their faces white. Hakim had scratched at the window a little while ago and Qasim had opened the shutters and let him in along with the helicopter pilot and the two guards who'd flown here with them.

Nobody said anything, but she could read rage in their eyes. She'd behaved stupidly and now they were all in danger.

"Qasim." She swallowed with difficulty. Her throat was so dry it felt parched. "He was going to—to touch my breast. I knew he was. And—"

"He was not going to touch your breast," Qasim snarled, swinging toward her. "It was an amusement for him. A test of wills between him and me. If you'd obeyed my orders—"

"That's easy for you to say. His slimy hands weren't on you!"

"If you'd obeyed my orders and hadn't drawn attention to yourself—"

"He's been staring at me for two days!"

Qasim felt a muscle knot in his jaw. Megan was right. He'd seen the son of a bitch watching her, but he'd told himself it was just an attempt to provoke him. Why would Ahmet, the most traditional of the tribal leaders, be interested in a foreigner?

He'd been the last to swear allegiance to Qasim after his father's death. Ever since, they'd played a game of wills.

How stupid he'd been, to think this was just another round.

"Why didn't you stop him when he put his arm around me?"

"What did you think I was doing?" Qasim said grimly. "You heard me talking to him. Didn't it occur to you I was telling him to take his hands off you?"

"You could have done more than tell him."

"It was a duel of wills." His mouth thinned. "He understood that if he touched you intimately, I'd have killed him."

"All that, in one little scene?" Megan snorted with contempt. "I think you have an overblown idea of your power, Sheikh Qasim."

"If I did," he said coldly, "Ahmet's men would have broken down that door twenty minutes ago. I'd be dead and what was left of you would be rotting in the desert."

The words rang with quiet conviction. Megan shuddered and wrapped her arms around herself.

"Then—then what do we do now?"

Qasim looked at her. She was pale, so pale that a tiny line of freckles he'd never noticed stood out clearly across the bridge of her nose. Her hair was a wild mass of curls framing her face. In the awful struggle in the meeting room, someone had half-torn off one of her sleeves, exposing the delicate curve of her arm.

Something seemed to expand inside his heart.

How beautiful she was. How brave. And how good she'd been, his Megan. He could only imagine what fortitude it had taken for her to play the part of a timid woman, sitting on that silly little stool, never speaking, never lifting her head, returning to this room in isolation each night and awakening each morning, knowing she had to pretend she was of no more importance than the walls.

He'd been proud of her...but he'd known it couldn't last.

And when she reacted to the pig who'd nudged her with his foot, he'd been torn between ordering her to behave and pulling her into his arms and kissing her.

You see? he'd longed to say, *this is what a woman should be like. Beautiful, and intelligent, and not afraid to speak her mind.*

He hadn't, of course. He had his nation to think of. He needed Ahmet's support for his plans. There was ore in these mountains and a small, painfully old-fashioned operation that mined it. He had plans already sketched out for a road, a small airport, a new smelter. None of it would destroy the vast, wild hills but would, instead, bring prosperity to a part of Suliyam that still lived with the poverty and diseases of ancient times.

And then Ahmet had touched her. Grabbed her wrist.

God, he'd wanted to kill him!

All that had stopped him was the cold realization that Ahmet's actions were part of a plan. The man wanted Megan, yes, but he wanted a confrontation with Qasim even more.

This was a test, then. Another grinding of will against will. He could not let Ahmet win, not with such high stakes. A fight here, where Ahmet ruled, and he'd die. Qasim had always known he might have to give his life for his country; he was prepared to do it, but not if it meant letting Ahmet and his followers impose their brand of cruel leadership on the rest of the kingdom...

Not if it meant letting him take Megan as a plaything.

So Qasim had forced himself to seem unruffled, even when Ahmet slid his meaty arm around Megan's waist.

Do not touch her, he'd said calmly. *It would not be wise.*

I think it would be, Ahmet had answered with a nasty smile.

It would not be, Qasim had told him. *I brought my people here in the spirit of friendship. Would you repudiate that friendship, Lord Ahmet? If so, you must also be prepared for the consequences.*

Check and mate, he'd thought, reading cold acquiescence in the man's face. One last dance of those meaty fingers, meant, Qasim knew, to save face...

And then Megan had taken matters into her own hands, and almost gotten both of them killed.

And he...hell, even as he'd figured he might have to fight his way out of the room, he'd felt his heart swell with pride at her courage.

How had this contrary female become so important to him in so short a time?

He turned toward her again. Her tear, like the tails of shooting stars, had left silvery streaks on her cheeks.

"Qasim?" she said in a whisper. "What do we do now?"

Qasim closed the distance between them in a few quick steps and gathered her gently into his arms. He heard Hakim's soft gasp, knew his men were staring, but he didn't give a damn.

For the first time since he'd ascended the throne, he was a man and not a king.

"Megan," he said softly, and when she lifted her face to his, he kissed her with all the tenderness in his heart. She sighed, leaned into his embrace and kissed him back.

"Stay here," he murmured, his lips an inch from hers. "Keep the door barred until I return."

"No! Qasim..."

He cupped her face and silenced her terrified protests with another kiss.

"I'll come back for you, *kalila*. I swear it."

She gave him a blurry smile. He brought her hands to his mouth and pressed kisses into the palms. Then he barked out a command to Hakim, to the pilot, to the two guards, unbarred the door and left the room.

CHAPTER EIGHT

DEAR God, what had she done?

Megan stood before one of the tall, narrow windows that looked over the mountains. Gray fog covered the barren plain, moving inexorably toward the walled city like a poisonous cloud.

Where are you, Qasim? Where are you?

Hours had gone by since the heavy wooden door had slammed behind him and still there was no word.

Time was moving as slowly as the fog. She felt helpless. Useless. The worst of it was that it was all her fault.

Qasim had warned her that working with him would be tough. *No problem,* she'd said, or words to that effect, and she'd glibly promised to follow all the demeaning rules of his country.

She'd been lying. To herself and to him.

What she'd really intended was to teach his people a thing or two about the proper role of women in civilized society.

Then they'd reached this awful place and she'd discovered that what he'd been trying to tell her was that parts of his kingdom had nothing to do with civilization as she knew it. And she'd done her best to keep her promise. She'd kept her mouth shut. She'd behaved.

If only she hadn't been forced to sit on that stool. If only Hakim hadn't acted like a self-important prig. If only Ahmet hadn't noticed her...

Damn it, why was she trying to come up with excuses?

Sure, those things had worked their way under her skin, but she'd been in the business world long enough to learn to roll with the punches. Her very first job with a prestigious firm, she'd traveled to Philadelphia with her boss. He'd stayed in an executive suite and arranged for her to have a connecting room.

"Makes things more convenient," he'd said, and she, innocent that she was, hadn't realized what that meant until she'd heard him rattling the doorknob in the middle of the night.

Meg? he'd called. *I have something here that will interest you.*

She'd lain frozen in silence, pretending she didn't hear him, and the next morning he'd acted as if nothing had happened and, damn it, so had she because she was afraid of losing her first really good job.

Lots of men still believed all it took was power to turn a woman into a conquest.

She could have dealt with the situation. She *should* have dealt with it, especially since Qasim had warned her.

What she couldn't deal with was the way Qasim had ignored her. Okay. Maybe he had no choice when they were with the others. She understood that. But that didn't explain why he hadn't found a minute to come to her room. Talk to her. Take her hand, as he had just before he'd ridden off with Ahmet's men. Tell her everything would be fine...

Megan closed her eyes.

Tell her he missed her. Wanted her. Longed for her, as she longed for him.

She turned from the window. She was thinking crazy thoughts, but didn't experts say that stress had weird effects on people? Hakim, for example, was standing like a statue in the same place he'd been when Qasim left.

She couldn't understand the aide's behavior. Why had he

let the man he called his master face whatever waited outside this door alone? Until now, Hakim had stayed at his heels like an obedient spaniel. Why had he abandoned him now?

Hakim swung toward her, eyes filled with hatred.

"I would never abandon my lord," he snarled, and Megan realized she'd spoken aloud.

"But you did. You let him face those barbarians all by himself!"

"The sheikh ordered me to stay here. I cannot disobey an order."

"Not even if it might save his life?"

"Obedience to him is not a matter of choice. You have no understanding of us, Miss O'Connell, or you would not question my actions."

"*You* have no understanding of what could be happening beyond that door, and damn your obedience!"

"Lord Qasim ordered me to watch over you." Hakim's mouth thinned. "I assure you, had I the power, I would not chose to do so."

"Oh, I'm sure of that. Why do you despise me, Hakim? I haven't done anything to you."

"You have bewitched the sheikh. He does not see it, but I do. You have clouded his thoughts."

"That's crazy!"

"He forgets that his duty is to Suliyam." Hakim came toward her, fists clenched at his sides. "Your witchcraft started when you wrote words in a document that made him want to change our way of life."

Megan threw out her hand, as if she were brushing aside a stinging insect. "You don't know what you're talking about. I made projections, estimated costs. Any changes for this—this godforsaken piece of earth come from Qasim, not me."

"And you show him disrespect. You refer to him by name, as if you were his equal."

"I *am* his equal," Megan snapped. "We don't scrape and bow to anyone in my world."

"That is the problem, Miss O'Connell. You think your world is the standard by which others must live, just as you think you know my lord. You do not! Soon, your witchcraft will wear off. You are only a female. In the end, his strength will be greater than any of your spells."

"I'm not going to listen to another—"

Hakim grabbed her arm. "You are a temporary diversion in the sheikh's life. Though he may bed you, I can promise that you'll never gain his heart."

"Touch me again," Megan said, grimacing as she twisted out of his grasp, "and I might just treat you to one of my so-called spells, you miserable old—"

A fist pounded against the door. Megan forgot Hakim, forgot everything when she heard Qasim's voice.

"Open up!"

Hakim started toward the door but she ran past him, slid the heavy bar free and flung the door wide.

"Qasim," she said happily, "Oh, thank God! I was afraid—"

"Nothing to be afraid of," Qasim said, and lurched sideways. "Nothing at…"

He fell toward her. Megan closed her arms around him but his weight was too much. The best she could manage was to slide slowly to the floor with him still in her arms.

"What did they do to you?" she whispered. "Qasim?"

"Caz," he said thickly, eyes closed and a loopy grin on his face. "You might as well call me…"

A snore rattled from his throat. Megan's eyebrows drew together. She bent over the man in her lap, sniffed…

"He's drunk," she said, looking up at Hakim in disbelief.

Hakim sighed. "That is good."

Good? It was good that Qasim had been drinking with his pals while she almost lost her mind imagining what had happened to him? That she'd been blaming herself for whatever awful fate had befallen him? That she'd been terrified she'd never see him again, never hear his voice, never feel his mouth on hers?

That such things had seemed to matter only made her angrier. She let Qasim's head down none-too-gently and shot to her feet.

"Be careful," Hakim snapped, rushing to ease a pillow under the sheikh's head.

"If this is good," Megan said grimly, "then you're right. I guess I really don't understand this country."

"It is not complicated."

"Oh, I think it is. Your sheikh goes off to be—to be drawn and quartered, and instead—"

"No one draws and quarters his enemies anymore," Hakim said, so seriously that she blinked. "Not even sheikh Ahmet." Hakim nodded toward the bed as he undid the top few buttons of Qasim's shirt. "Get that blanket."

She wanted to tell him to get it himself, but why play the role of sullen child? She was angry enough not to give a damn if Qasim froze to death, but she yanked the blanket from the bed and dropped it over him.

So much for thinking he'd been defending her or worried about her.

"There." Hakim waved his hand to the other men as he rose to his feet. "We will leave you now, Miss O'Connell."

"That's fine. Just don't think you can go without taking your sheikh with you."

"His highness will probably sleep for several hours. You may send for me when he awakens."

"Wait just a damned minute! You've got it wrong, pal.

You may call *me* when he awakens, and only so I can tell your fearless leader what I think of him."

"Sheikh Qasim drank with Sheikh Ahmet."

Megan folded her arms and smiled with her teeth. "A brilliant deduction."

"That means they held a successful negotiation."

She looked down at Qasim. He'd rolled onto his side and was sleeping soundly as a baby.

"How? By drinking each other under the table?"

"They drank," Hakim said coldly, "because they solved their differences. That is how it was done in the old days. And, in the old days, to drink less than the man who was your enemy was to insult him."

"In other words, what we see here is an example of good manners."

Hakim nodded. "It is so."

"Good manners," Megan said again, and rolled her eyes. Would she ever make sense of any of this? Still, the threat to their safety was over. She could, she supposed, let Qasim sleep it off on the floor. It was only that she felt a knot of anger each time she looked at him. No matter what Hakim said, the negotiations couldn't have been very difficult, not if they ended in a party.

"Miss O'Connell? You will send for me when my lord awakens."

"With pleasure."

She took a chair to the window, carefully placed it so her back would face Qasim, and sat down. She heard the door shut; after a minute, despite what Hakim had said about successful negotiations, she went to it and slid the heavy bar into place.

Qasim was still sleeping. Caz. He'd told her to call him Caz.

She looked down at him again, at the thick, dark lashes

lying against his tanned skin. He looked peaceful, content, not at all concerned at how she'd worried…

At the anguish she'd suffered, imagining him hurt or dead.

Megan rose to her feet. She knelt next to Qasim, stroked his hair back from his forehead, and touched her hand to his cheek.

"I'm glad you're safe," she whispered. "Very, very glad."

Gently she brushed her lips over his.

Then she sat by the window, stared out at the fog-shrouded plain and wondered what was happening to her because something was, something she didn't understand, didn't want, had never wanted.

When darkness came, she lay her head back and drifted off to sleep.

Caz came awake all at once, heart pounding, fighting his way out of a nightmare that involved himself, Ahmet and a room choked with the stench of alcohol.

He blinked, forced his eyes open, and groaned. Bloody hell. He was lying on the floor. What…?

And then he remembered. Ahmet. His unbelievable demand. His response. The endless hours of finding a way out of a situation that could, in an instant, turn into disaster…and then the solution and the glass after glass of a clear liquid that had the smell of rotten potatoes and the kick of a mule.

His head felt as if it were going to explode. Slowly, carefully, he sat up and looked around him. A single oil lamp flickered on a low table. This room wasn't his. It was Megan's. Yes, he saw her now, asleep in a big chair near the window.

His heart turned over as he thought of what he had to tell

her. How would she deal with it? She was brave—he'd never known a woman with more courage. And she was intelligent. With luck, she'd understand what he'd done, why he'd done it, that he had no choice and neither did she. Yes, she'd say, of course, I'll do it if I must.

She might even lift her arms to him, whisper that it wasn't such an awful fate, that what they had to do might be—might be—

"Idiot," Caz mumbled, and tore his eyes from her.

Megan wouldn't tell him anything but what he deserved. She'd say he was an arrogant fool for having gotten her into this mess, but she'd agree to the terms he'd set.

It wasn't as if either of them had a choice.

He took a steadying breath and got to his feet. A red-hot lance of pain drove through his skull. There had to be a way to clear his head. He had to, before he told Megan that they—that he and she…

Black coffee. There was an earthenware pot of it on the table. It was cold and would probably taste like old socks, but he needed caffeine and to hell with the taste. Sugar, too. That would help. Caz filled a cup with viscous black liquid, added six misshapen lumps of raw sugar, stirred the resultant mess and slugged it down. He gagged on the last mouthful but a couple of deep breaths helped keep the stuff in his gut. Then he poured another cup and went through the whole process again.

Better. Much better. Damn, what he'd give for a shower.

His eyes fell on the pitcher and basin that stood on a small table in the far corner. One quick glance at Megan. Yes, she was still sleeping. Quickly Caz unbuttoned his shirt, unzipped his trousers, kicked off his leather boots, stripped down to his skin. He took a mouthful of the water—God, it was cold—and spat it into the basin. Then he gritted his teeth, raised the pitcher and dumped the contents over his head.

God!

His teeth banged together like castanets; he shuddered from his head straight down to his toes, but the coffee, sugar and icy water combined did the trick. He was stone cold sober and the pain in his head was almost—*almost*—bearable.

He dressed quickly, wishing he could put on stuff that didn't bear the lingering scent of the rotgut he'd had to swallow to convince Ahmet it wouldn't be wise to screw with him. Going toe to toe, matching him drink for drink, had been the only way to deal with the ugly son of a bitch.

Caz ran his hands through his wet hair, shoving it back from his face.

Okay. He was as ready as he'd ever be. It was time to wake Megan and explain the devil's bargain he'd made.

He made his way quietly across the carpeted floor, paused beside her chair and looked down at her. Her head was thrown back; her lashes lay against her cheek. Her pulse beat slowly and steadily in the hollow of her throat. He had kissed her there; he remembered the sweet taste of her flesh, the erotic whisper of her heartbeat against his lips.

Yes, she was beautiful and bright and courageous, but how had she gotten under his skin in so short a time? He'd known lots of women, had many lovers, been with a couple of them for months, but none had ever stirred his emotions this way. As often as he'd wanted to turn Megan over his knee and teach her some manners, he'd wanted to take her in his arms and make love to her.

And sometimes, sometimes it was enough just to know she was in the same room, that he could look over and see her face, enough to know she was part of his life…

A chill danced down his spine.

Amazing, what effect stress could have on a man, he thought, and hunched down beside the chair.

"Megan."

She didn't stir.

"Megan," he said briskly, "wake up."

Her lashes fluttered, the lids rose. She stared at him, her eyes dark and unseeing, and then a smile flickered across her mouth.

"Caz," she whispered, and he stopped trying to treat this as just another moment in his life, stopped trying to figure out what in hell was happening to him, whispered her name, bent his head to hers and kissed her.

Her mouth was sweet and soft, and when she sighed, he drew her breath in, let it mix with his. She moaned and he curved his arm around her, drew her close and deepened the kiss. A long time later, he drew back, looked into her eyes and brushed her sleep-tousled hair from her temple.

"Hello, *kalila*," he whispered.

"You're awake."

He laughed softly. "Yes."

She touched his hair. It was damp. "Were you outside? Is it raining?"

He took her hand, pressed it to his lips. "I took a shower. Well, I took what passes for a shower in this place. I'm afraid I used up all your water."

A picture flashed through her mind. Qasim, tall, proud, naked. "Here?"

"You were asleep."

"The last time I saw you, you were passed out on the floor."

His smile dimmed. "I'm sure I was."

"You were drunk."

"I know, *kalila*. I'm so sorry, but—"

"And you asked me to call you 'Caz.'"

"Did I?"

She nodded. "It is a nickname?"

"My roommate dubbed me 'Caz' my first semester at Yale, and it seemed a lot more American than Qasim, so from then on, that's what I called myself."

Megan traced the tip of her finger along his mouth. In the dark, with only the soft light of the oil lamp for illumination, with the silence of the mountains all around them, anything seemed right…and she'd wanted to touch her finger to his mouth for a long time, to follow those soft curves that could spark such excitement. She knew she should be angry at him for abandoning her and getting drunk, but right now she could only think how good it felt to be in his arms.

"Ah," she said softly, with the hint of a smile. "You didn't mind being a little bit American then."

"I never minded it. My mother was American." His smile tilted. "I liked her country far more than she liked mine."

"What happened to her?"

"She couldn't adapt to life in Suliyam and she went home."

"Without you?"

"Without me. Don't look so sad, *kalila*. Really, I had a happy childhood."

"Then why do you look so sad when you mention her?"

"Do I look sad?" Caz brought her hand to his mouth again. "It must be the light." He cleared his throat, and she knew he was going to change the topic. "We can talk about this another time, Megan. Right now…right now, we have another matter to discuss."

"Yes. We certainly do."

Her tone had changed. Well, he could hardly blame her for being angry, and he told her so.

"I don't blame you for being upset."

"Upset?" She pulled away from him and rose to her feet. "I wasn't upset," she lied. "I just think you could have found a way to let me know you weren't being murdered."

"I'm sorry, *kalila*. But there was no time."

"I imagined the most awful things, Caz. Terrible things."

"Sweetheart." Caz stood up and reached for her hand. "Forgive me for putting you through this."

His expression was contrite. She thought of her role in all this, and her anger faded as swiftly as it had taken hold.

"It's my fault," she said softly. "I made a mess of things."

"No!" Caz gathered her in his arms. "I should never have brought you to these mountains. I should have seen through Ahmet's lies. He wasn't ill, he only wanted me to bend to him. And, like a fool, I did." He paused. "But you're right. Awful things might have happened. They won't," he added quickly. "I promise."

Megan laid her hands on Caz's chest. She could feel the steady beat of his heart beneath her palms.

"I thought of what he might do to you." Her voice shook. "Caz, I thought—"

"Ahmet behaves like an animal when it suits him, but he's not a fool. He wouldn't harm me. He knows the other tribes would avenge my death and show him no mercy."

She laughed shakily. "And here I thought he was going to feed you to a pack of hungry wolves."

"You've seen too many bad movies, *kalila*," Caz said softly. "In fact, he went out of his way to be…gracious."

"There's a word I'd never use for him."

"You impressed him, Megan."

"I'll just bet," she said, with a little laugh. "He'd probably like to toss me off the top of a mountain."

"On the contrary. He finds you interesting."

"I'm sure there's a less polite word to describe it."

"He says he's never known a woman like you. And he's right."

Caz's eyes were like flame on her mouth. She felt her lips soften, her muscles turning liquid in sweet anticipation of his kiss, but he didn't kiss her. Instead he circled her wrists with his hands and drew back.

"We have a problem," he said quietly.

In an instant, the mood in the darkened room had changed. Megan stared at Caz and the expression on his face chilled her to the bone.

"A problem?"

"Ahmet wants…something."

"What?"

"He wants you."

"What?" She forced a laugh. This had to be a joke but Caz wasn't laughing. He wasn't even smiling. She could feel the color drain from her face. "What do you mean, he wants—"

"He wants to take you as his wife."

"Well, that's—that's…" Her stomach lurched. "You told him, of course, I'd never—that I would never, ever—"

She cried out as Caz clasped her shoulders and lifted her to her toes. "Listen to me, Megan. As he sees it, he's offered you a great honor." His voice softened. "Don't look like that, *kalila*. Do you think I would let this happen? He's not going to have you."

Megan slumped against him. "For a minute, I thought… But Hakim said things had gone well. He said that was why you'd had so much to drink. He said—"

"He probably said it was tradition. A word you've come to despise—and, in this instance, one I do, too." Caz shuddered. "I'd much rather celebrate with a handshake than with cups of horse piss." The muscle in his jaw tightened.

So did the grip of his hands on her. "But it was worth it. You see, I found the one reason Ahmet can't have you."

Megan smiled. "I'll bet it was creative."

"It was." He paused. "I told him that you couldn't very well marry him when you were already promised to me."

CHAPTER NINE

SILENCE. What was called a pregnant pause in bad novels, Megan thought wildly, but what could a woman say to a man after he'd just told her...after he'd said that she...that he...

Maybe she'd misunderstood.

"You told Ahmet," she said carefully, "that I couldn't marry him because—"

"—because you're going to marry me."

She waited for Caz to add something. When he didn't, she nodded as if what he'd told her made absolute sense.

"Oh."

"Is that all you have to say, *kalila?* Nothing but 'oh'?"

Caz sounded annoyed. Annoyed? At her? For saying "oh" after hearing him say—

The room shifted out of focus. Caz tightened his hold on her wrists.

"Megan?" His voice was sharp. "Are you all right?"

"Yes. Yes, I'm..." She cleared her throat. "Actually I'm surprised."

His smile was quick and wolfish. "I don't doubt it."

"That you'd have to come up with such a lie, I mean. You're the ruler of this kingdom. Ahmet is your subject. Surely you can simply tell him that what he wants is out of the question."

"I did."

"Well, then—"

"He laughed."

"I really don't follow this, Caz. You told him he couldn't—that he can't take me for his wife and he laughed?"

Caz let go of her. He dug his hands into his pockets and began pacing the room. He'd known this wouldn't be easy. How could a man explain ancient customs of the east to a woman of the twenty-first century west? Ahmet and his followers were the last of his people whose feet were firmly planted in the past. Moving them forward required a deft touch. His father had proven that; he'd tried to institute change through royal decree and it had only led to bloodshed.

Besides, a royal decree was impossible without the force to back it. Caz had deliberately come to these mountains without a show of arms. He'd meant it as a good faith gesture, but now his plan was about to backfire.

And bringing Megan with him had been another error. He'd figured it would present some problems. What he hadn't anticipated was that Megan would be a temptation to a man like Ahmet.

Now, Megan's fate was in his hands. Her fate, and the fate of this peace mission. One false step and Ahmet would surely decide to take what he wanted and the consequences be damned.

If that happened, Megan's future, and Suliyam's, might both be lost.

"Answer me, damn it," Megan demanded. "How can Ahmet even think he can get away with something like this? All you have to do is say 'no!'"

Caz turned to her. Her stance said she was ready to take on the world, shoulders back, chin up, eyes bright with defiance...and yet, he could see something beyond all that.

Fear.

What a fool he was, he thought angrily, and he crossed the room in a few quick strides and caught her in his arms.

"I *have* told him 'no,'" he said quietly. "And given him a reason why he must accept my decision." He tightened his hold on her, lifted her to her toes so she had no choice but to look into his eyes. "Telling him he can't have you wouldn't ensure your safety. The situation is complex but you have to trust me, *kalila*. Now that I've said you are to be my wife, you're safe."

"And I have nothing to say about it?"

"No," Caz said sharply. "Not unless you like the idea of having Ahmet as your husband."

"Don't be ridiculous! I'd never—"

"Then stop arguing, damn it! Why make such a fuss?"

Why, indeed? Megan thought. Caz had lied about their relationship. So what? Why this hollow feeling inside? Someday, this would make a great story. *And then there was the time I was in this little country in the middle of nowhere,* she'd say, *and the guy who ruled it had to pretend he wanted to make me his wife...*

"You're right," she said, forcing a smile to her lips. "What you did was creative. Heck, it's brilliant. Ahmet's a barbarian, but not even he would be foolish enough to try and steal his king's fiancée."

Part two, coming up, Caz thought grimly, and cleared his throat. "Unfortunately, he still might."

"But—but you just said..."

"It isn't enough."

"It isn't?" Megan shook her head. "You're losing me, Caz. Didn't you just tell me that I was safe? That now that Ahmet knows we're—that he knows, he has to accept defeat?"

"Being betrothed isn't the same as being wed."

Such formal words, so calmly spoken. He might have

been discussing the weather. Was she the only one who found the prospect of a phony engagement disturbing?

"Why not? He'll never know that we aren't really going to—"

"Of course he will," Caz said impatiently. "I know you think you've stepped into a time warp, but news travels here the same as it does in your world."

"Why are you putting words in my mouth? I don't think that. I'm sure not everyone's like Ahmet."

"Yeah." Caz nodded. "I'm sorry, *kalila*. I'm a little edgy."

"Well, so am I. It isn't every day I become engaged, especially to a sheikh."

Megan smiled, to make sure he understood she was joking, but he didn't return the smile. Instead his expression became grim.

"You might as well prepare yourself for another shock."

"What shock? Why are you looking at me like that?" Her heart seemed to turn over. "Caz? What is it?"

"Ahmet may be a brute, but he isn't stupid. Do you think he'd let you go just because I suddenly announced our engagement?" He moved closer to her, his eyes locked to hers. "He wants to give us a gift."

"What kind of—"

"A wedding," Caz said, his tone flat. "He offered to have our marriage take place here. Today."

"And you said…" Her voice was scratchy. She cleared her throat and began again. "And you said, 'thank you, but—'"

"And I said we would be delighted to have the ceremony here, in these magnificent mountains."

Megan stared at him in stunned disbelief, waiting for him to smile and say it was all a joke, but his steady gaze assured her that he'd meant every word.

"No!"

"You can't say 'no,' Megan. I thought I made that clear."

"I can say whatever I like, and my answer is—"

Caz caught her by the shoulders.

"I have not *asked* you to marry me," he said brusquely, "I've *told* you to marry me. There's a world of difference."

"You're insane! You can't tell me—"

"Yes," he said harshly, I can. I am the ruler of this country. My word is law."

There it was, the true nature of the Sheikh of Suliyam. He was a dictator and she, fool that she was, had done everything she could not to acknowledge that truth.

"Not in my world, it isn't. You can't force me to—"

She cried out as his hands bit into her flesh. "The world you know has no meaning here. Would you prefer to see the few men I brought with me slaughtered?" He lowered his head until his eyes burned into hers. "My men's lives are worth more to me than your foolish female pride."

"And me?" she said, in a papery whisper. "What am I worth to you?"

His mouth twisted. What he'd just told her was true enough, but it wasn't all of it. His men were prepared to give their lives for him, and he had been raised to willingly give his life for his people.

But when Ahmet leered at him and said he wanted Megan, he hadn't thought about his men first, or his people, or his responsibility to the throne.

He'd thought of Megan, lying beneath Ahmet's savage bulk. Of the barbarian's hands on her. Of her tears, her terror, and he'd come as close to insanity as a man could get without tumbling over the edge.

His hands had knotted into fists; his heart pounded. He'd looked into Ahmet's fat, ugly face and imagined it bloodied beyond repair, imagined the joy of beating him to his knees...

He'd reached deep inside himself, struggled to hold on to reason even as his vision reddened, and acknowledged that if he attacked the barbarian, he'd surely seal Megan's fate.

Could he tell her that? Tell her that he would gladly give his life for hers, if he thought it would save her? No. He couldn't. Such a thought was irrational and he couldn't afford to be irrational.

He was the king.

"You're very important to me," he said carefully. "I'm responsible for your welfare." She seemed to sag in his hands. What more did she want him to say? Caz searched for the words that would make this easier and finally found them. "Of course, the marriage won't be real."

Her head came up and she looked into his eyes. "It won't?"

"The ceremony will have meaning only in Suliyam, not in the States. I'll take care of nullifying it on my end. You won't have to do anything to set it aside."

"Oh. I didn't... I thought..."

"We'll return to the palace tomorrow, I'll put you on a plane and send you home." His voice, and his hands, gentled. "And then you can put what happened here out of your mind."

Put it out of her mind. She'd exchange wedding vows, then put them out of her mind?

"Megan? Do you see how simple this is?"

She looked at Caz again. His gray eyes were steady on hers. He looked like a man who'd just suggested an appropriate dinner menu instead of a marriage, calm and pleasant...except for a tiny flicker of muscle beating in his jaw.

"It isn't as if the ceremony will have any real meaning."

"No. I understand that now."

"All you'll have to do is play the part of obedient female a little longer." Caz's voice roughened. "Obedient, and eager."

"Excuse me?"

"Ahmet wondered why I hadn't married you already. It was an excellent question, and I answered by telling him I'd wanted to wait until I could plan an extravagant celebration but that being alone with you these past days had been difficult for me. For you, as well." Caz slid one hand up her throat; he could feel Megan's pulse drumming beneath his fingers. "A man doesn't sleep with the woman he intends to wed," he said huskily.

Megan nodded. It all made perfect sense. Her head told her so. Her heart was the part of her having a problem. She'd never really thought about marriage but surely if you did decided to say "I do," it was supposed to have some meaning.

Wasn't it?

Weren't you supposed to look at the man you were marrying and feel giddy with excitement? Weren't you supposed to want his kisses? Weren't you supposed to want to be with him all the time, to talk to him and yes, argue with him, and laugh with him…and feel everything she felt for Qasim?

The room tilted. Caz tightened his hold on her.

"*Kalila*. Don't be afraid. I won't let anything happen to you."

Something was happening already, but how could she tell him that?

"Besides," he added softly, "we have no choice."

His eyes darkened; his gaze fell to her mouth. Later, she would wonder who made the first move, she or he. Not that it mattered. His kiss consumed her, burned away what little remained of reason and replaced it with his taste, his scent, his strength.

Shaken, she stepped back.

"No choice at all," he said, and left her.

Time slowed to a tortoise's pace.

Caz didn't come back. She hadn't expected him to. Wasn't there some tradition about a bridegroom not seeing his bride on their wedding day?

And wasn't that a sad attempt at humor? Megan thought, as she paced back and forth. She wasn't a bride and Caz wasn't her groom. They were two people trapped in a nasty game of treachery, and the sooner they got things finished here, the better.

The one person she half expected to see was Hakim, coming to demand she not go through with the wedding...but why would he do that? Hakim would know, as she did, that the next few hours would be a farce.

In midmorning, her serving women showed up with platters of food and pitchers of fruit juice. Their sullen expressions were gone. Now, they approached her with their eyes cast down.

Megan waved the food and drink away. One mouthful of anything and her stomach would revolt. Farce or not, it wasn't every day she stood at an altar and said "I do."

The women sat down and watched her. They giggled and whispered to each other. They shot her little looks filled with meaning, poked each other in the ribs and giggled again. She'd gone to enough bridal showers to know what was going on.

"Trust me," she said, "it's not like that."

The youngest of them drew a deep breath. For courage, obviously, because a few seconds later, she spoke.

"The sheikh is very handsome."

Megan raised her eyebrows. "You speak English?"

"The sheikh is very handsome."

Megan hunched down in front of the girl. "Tell me, please, what will the wedding be like?"

"The sheikh is very—"

"Handsome," Megan said glumly, and rose to her feet.

So much for speaking English. So much for finding out what lay ahead. So much for anything, except pacing and pacing, and telling herself this would all be over in a little while.

This wasn't the way a bride was supposed to feel.

Not that she'd ever thought much about being a bride. Why would any woman want to give up her life?

That was what you had to do, even if the books said you didn't, even if her oh-so-independent big sister had taken the plunge. Fallon might have forgotten the great lesson of their childhood. She hadn't. She'd grown up watching their mother put aside her own needs for her husband's pleasure. Mary would settle into a new place, start turning a usually decrepit four walls into a home, make a few friends and then Pop would come home one night, filled with enthusiasm for some new get-rich-quick scheme, and announce that it was time to move on.

What men wanted always came first. That was just the way it was. Some women were okay with it, but she wasn't one of them.

Wasn't it a damned good thing this marriage would only be a sham?

She looked out the window, where trails of fog wound around the stunted scrub as they had last night.

Twenty-four hours, and nothing had changed.

Twenty-four hours, and everything had changed.

Real or not, nothing would be the same after tonight. She had the weirdest feeling, as if someone had popped the cork on a bottle of champagne and the bubbles were effervescing in her blood.

What if the wedding were real? There was no harm in imagining that. What if Caz had come to her and said, *Don't think. Don't ask questions. Don't ask for logic, because there isn't any. I only know that I want you more than life itself. Marry me, Megan. Stay with me forever.*

What would her answer have been?

No, of course.

That's what she'd have told him, wasn't it? Or would she have gone into his arms, forgotten what she knew of marriage, forgotten that she knew this man only a handful of days.

Would she have brought his mouth down to hers, whispered her answer against the warmth of his lips?

Her throat constricted. She swung around and stared at the silent women.

"I can't do this," she said. "I can't—"

The door swung open. Two more servants bustled into the room, hands and arms filled with silks and cashmeres and jewels.

Megan turned to the girl who'd spoken those half dozen words of English.

"Help me," she begged. "Please, get me out of here! I don't want to marry the sheikh. I can't—"

The women descended on her like wolves on a lamb. Megan shrieked, struck out in desperation, but there were eight of them and one of her. They stripped her of her clothes, dumped her in a wooden tub that appeared as if by magic, washed her body, her hair, dried and perfumed her.

"Stop it," she kept saying, "damn you, keep your hands off me!"

Maybe they thought it was a game. Maybe tradition said the bride was supposed to put up a fight. Nobody listened, nobody paid attention, nobody even spoke to her until she was dressed and hung with jewels.

Then the two eldest women dragged her in front of the full-length mirror that had appeared at the same time as the tub.

"Look," the youngest woman, the one who'd pretended not to speak English, said.

Megan looked. And stared at what she saw.

The glass was old. Some of the silver backing had worn off; in other places, her reflection seemed to shimmer like waves on the sea.

But the image was clear enough to make her catch her breath.

Looking back at her was a stranger, a seductive creature draped in jewels that were ancient and beautiful, her hair woven with flowers, her body draped in royal-blue silk.

Something old, she thought giddily, *something new, something borrowed, something blue.*

"You see?" the youngest of the women whispered.

Yes. Yes, she saw. They had changed her. Megan O'Connell was gone. In her place was—

"The sheikh's bride," the young woman whispered.

Less than an hour later, that was who she became.

The ceremony was long and probably beautiful.

If she'd been watching it in a travel film, that's how she'd have described it. An enormous room lit by candles. A pathway, strewn with rose petals. An altar. A canopy, at any rate, made of royal blue silk shot with gold.

And Caz, waiting for her. Caz, in a white silk shirt and black breeches with riding boots the color of the night. Caz, his face serious, his eyes locked to hers. Words spoken by Ahmet, who'd managed to look human for the occasion. Caz's husky responses, her choked "Yes" when he told her it was time to say the word. And then a roar went up from the throats of Ahmet's men, and Caz's arms went around her, and the roar grew louder as he crushed her mouth beneath his.

"You are my wife," he said softly, and she told herself it was all a game even as her arms went around his neck and she drew his head to hers for another deep, deep kiss.

Hands reached for her. Women's hands. Laughing, they dragged her away, surrounded her, tugged her along with them while the men did the same thing to Caz. The women brought her to another room, seated her on an intricately carved chair that stood on a high platform. The men seated Caz beside her. Music—the hot beat of drums, the haunting cry of a flute—filled the room.

The women danced. The men strutted. There were platters of food and endless glasses filled with a liquid that had no color.

"Don't even take a sip," Caz said, leaning toward her.

Megan looked at him. My husband, she thought. He's my husband. "Poison?" she whispered.

"Of a sort," he said solemnly. "It's what got me so polluted last night."

He grinned. She laughed. How strange, to hear such an American word in such a foreign setting. To hear the word on her husband's lips.

"Stand up, sweetheart."

"Why?"

"It's time for us to leave."

To leave. To be alone with this man who she'd just married. Her heart bumped again. "Won't that be rude? Ahmet might think—"

"Are you afraid to be alone with me?"

She was afraid of what she was feeling, but how could she tell him that?

"No, certainly not. I just—"

Caz rose to his feet and reached for her, lifting her from her chair and high into his arms. A roar went up from the crowd. She felt a rush of heat along her skin; she wound her arms around his neck and buried her face against his throat as he strode from the room.

"Hold tight, *kalila*," he said softly, and she did, clinging to him, inhaling his scent until she was dizzy with it as he crossed the floor, climbed and climbed and climbed a staircase that she thought might be winding its way to heaven.

Hakim called out to them. "My lord! Lord Qasim!"

"Leave us," Caz growled.

"But my lord..."

Megan lifted her head. They had reached a narrow landing. Hakim stood halfway down the steep staircase. His eyes met hers and the hatred she saw in them made her catch her breath.

A massive wooden door loomed ahead. Caz shouldered it open, then kicked it shut behind him.

They were alone.

She knew it even before he slid her slowly down the length of his body and stood her on her feet. All she could hear was the beat of her heart and the snap of logs blazing on an enormous stone hearth.

Slowly she looked around her. They were in a silk-draped room lit by hundreds of white candles. The sole furnishing was a bed draped in sheer white linen and piled high with silk blankets and pillows.

"Megan."

Caz put his hand under her chin and lifted it. "It's all done now, sweetheart," he said softly. "Nobody's watching us. You can relax."

Relax? She almost laughed. Or cried. It was hard to know which was the better choice.

"Megan? Are you all right?"

"Fine," she said briskly. "I just... It's been a difficult day, you know?"

He knew. She'd begun the day an outcast, a modern-day Rapunzel locked away in the castle of a wicked magician, and ended it the wife of a sheikh.

His wife.

His pretend wife. He had to keep remembering that. The ceremony had been real enough, for Ahmet's people. Real enough for him, had he chosen to let it be so, but that didn't mean they were actually bound together in marriage.

The words they'd spoken weren't in his wife's language. The ceremony wasn't part of his wife's culture.

He wasn't the man his wife would have chosen for her husband.

And, damn it, she wasn't his wife.

How come he kept forgetting that?

Caz took a deep breath, then exhaled it slowly. Because he wanted her, that was how come. He'd wanted her from the first time he'd set eyes on her, sharp tongue, fiery temper and all. And now she was his.

How was a man supposed to remember he had no right to touch his bride on their wedding night? The moon was climbing the sky, casting its shy light through the window. The fire was as hot as his blood, the bed an invitation. He imagined what it would be like to undress her by the light of all those candles, watch as they cast shadows on her skin, as he exposed her to his eyes...

Hell.

Caz swung away. He was a man of discipline. A sheikh who had long ago learned to ignore his own needs when he had to. Surely, he could keep his hands off his wife for one night.

His wife, he thought again, and he knotted his hands, dug

them deep into his trouser pockets and walked to the far side of the room, deliberately putting as much distance as possible between himself and the woman he could not think of as his bride.

"All right," he said briskly. "I'll take some of those blankets and pillows and make myself a bed on the floor."

"You don't have to. I trust you. You can sleep…"

"No," he said sharply. "That wasn't part of our deal. I'll sleep on the floor. You sleep in the bed. And at first light, I'll take you away from here. All this will be over, Megan. We won't have to pretend this is the way we wanted things to be."

He almost told her more. That if he lay down in that bed with her, nothing would keep him from taking her.

But this was a charade. She wasn't his. She never could be.

So he tossed some pillows and blankets on the floor, went from candle to candle, snuffing out all but half a dozen nearest the bed so she wouldn't be trapped in the dark. Then he got beneath the blankets and turned his back to her.

"Get some sleep," he said gruffly. "You need it."

She didn't answer, but he hadn't expected her to. By now, she was probably terrified. The strange ceremony. The wild dancing. All of it must have struck her as barbaric.

Caz heard the whisper of silk, the creak of the mattress and shut his eyes to the images that danced through his head. His bride was in bed. He was on the floor. Damn Ahmet, anyway. Damn tradition, and custom, and the world itself.

What good was a kingdom when what a man wanted was—when the only thing he wanted was…

His wife.

CHAPTER TEN

HE HADN'T thought he could sleep but exhaustion reached up, dragged him down into the darkness.

Caz slept. He *must* have slept, because the next thing he knew, the few candles still lit were sputtering, moonlight filled the room...

And his wife stood by the window, weeping.

Caz was off the floor in a heartbeat. "Sweetheart?"

She kept her back to him, shook her head and fluttered her hands in that way women had of saying *Don't, stay away, I'm fine.* But he didn't believe it, not for a minute, and when he reached her, he took her gently by the shoulders and turned her to him.

"*Kalila*. What is it?"

Megan looked up. Moonlight striped Caz's face; she saw herself reflected in his pupils, a small, pathetic woman crying as if her heart might break, and for what reason? He'd done exactly as he'd promised. Saved her from Ahmet by marrying her, by pretending a wedding was what he'd wanted, by carrying her from the hall in the sight of hundreds of cheering barbarians and bringing her to this beautiful room...

To what should have been her wedding night.

The man she'd married was a man of his word. He'd done all he'd said he would...and her heart was breaking. Until this moment, she hadn't been brave enough to face the reason. Now, in that deepest time of night when truth is all that matters, she understood her despair.

She hadn't wanted Caz to bring her here and treat her honorably. She'd wanted him to lock the door, take her in his arms, tell her he was going to make her his wife.

"Megan."

His voice was ragged as their eyes met. Her heart began to race. Could he read her thoughts? What could be more humiliating than to have him realize that she wanted him?

"Megan," he said again, in a velvet whisper, and he lowered his mouth to hers and kissed her.

His kiss was soft; his touch gentle. He held her as if she were made of glass.

Still, she wept.

"Don't cry, *kalila.* I won't let anything hurt you."

He wouldn't, not if he lost his life defending her. She was safe now, but he knew what it had cost her. He'd put her through hell, brought her into the lair of a barbarian, forced her into marriage.

When you came down to it, how much difference was there between him and Ahmet?

But she'd accepted his kiss, even moved closer to him, her body pressed to his, taking comfort from his strength.

He rocked her against him, whispered words to soothe her in his own tongue.

She smelled of flowers, night and woman. Caz shut his eyes, buried his face in her hair, let her scent fill him.

His mouth twisted with irony.

His bride was clinging to him because he was the only familiar thing in her life, and he could only think how incredible it felt to hold her...

And how badly he wanted her.

So badly that he was going to give himself away, if he let her lean against him much longer.

Carefully he clasped her shoulders and tried to put some space between them. Megan shook her head and burrowed closer.

"It's okay," he murmured. "You're safe. I'll always keep you safe."

She sighed. He felt the flutter of her breath on his skin. Caz swallowed hard and reminded himself that this was all about offering comfort.

"Shall I get you a drink of water? Some coffee? I can slip downstairs…"

"Coffee's the last thing I need right now," she said with a little laugh. "Please, just—just stay with me."

Megan slipped her arms around his waist. Her cheek pressed against his chest. God, what was she doing to him? He had to think about something else. The night. Tomorrow's weather. Would it be okay? The helicopter…

"Caz?"

"What?"

"I'm sorry."

She was sorry? He held her away from him again, just enough so he could see her face. "For what?"

"Everything. I screwed up your meeting."

He smiled. "Livened it up, you mean."

"And I've put you at odds with Ahmet."

"I've always been at odds with Ahmet."

"Yes, but now… Is he angry? Because you and I are…because he thinks you and I are…"

"On the contrary." His smile tilted. "He's gained respect for me. I've got the girl he wanted."

That put an answering smile on her face.

"Better?" he said softly.

She nodded.

"No more tears, then." He plucked a silk scarf from the

back of a chair and gently blotted her eyes. "A woman shouldn't weep on her wedding night."

"Actually..." She gave a little laugh. "Actually that's the reason I was crying."

"I understand. When you agreed to come to Suliyam with me, you never imagined you'd end up being forced into marriage with a stranger."

"You're not a stranger," Megan said quickly. "In some ways, I feel as if I've known you all my life." She took a breath. "I was crying because I was thinking back a few weeks. One of my brothers just got married and the ceremony was, you know, filled with emotion."

"Ah. I understand. Our ceremony had to be an alien—"

She silenced him by putting her fingers lightly across his mouth. "You don't understand." Her voice softened. "It was a wonderful ceremony."

Caz's eyebrows rose. "Yeah?"

She smiled. A minute ago, he'd sounded like the exalted sheikh of Suliyam. Now, he sounded like a guy she might have met in the States.

"Yeah," she said gently. "The words that sounded so solemn, the bells, the dancers, and then, at the end, all those people sending up that wild cry..."

"They were happy for us."

"I know." Her smile dimmed. "And that's why I was crying, you know? I thought of how happy everyone was at my brother's wedding, and how happy they were at our— at the wedding today, and I felt, I don't know, guilty, maybe, because what happened wasn't real and..."

"You're a good and generous woman, Megan O'Connell."

"I'm a woman who's complicated your life."

Caz tilted her face up to his. "You've enriched it," he

said softly. "And you honored me enormously by becoming my bride."

"I am, aren't I?" Megan whispered. She could feel her blood humming. "Your bride, Caz. Your bride for this night."

They stared at each other. The sounds of the night, the sigh of the wind…everything faded away. There was nothing on the earth but this room. This moment.

"Caz?" Her voice flowed over him like liquid silver. "Do you want me?"

"Want you?" He made a sound that was half groan, half laugh. "*Kalila,* you're all I think about. You fill my mind, my soul, my heart."

"Then take me, Caz. Make me your wife tonight."

He looked down into her face and thought of a dozen reasons to kiss her and put her from him, to walk out of here and into the chill mountain night. He was a king. A man of honor.

But he'd never wanted a woman as he wanted her. And on this one night, he would be a man, not a king.

A man who would make love to his bride.

He gathered her into his arms and took her mouth with his. She moaned his name and wound her arms around his neck.

"I want to taste you, *kalila.* Every part of you."

Oh yes. It was what she wanted, too. All the arguing. The battle of words and will. Had it all been pretence to hide the truth? She sighed as Caz kissed her mouth, bent and nipped at her throat, brushed his lips over the straining silk that covered her breasts.

How could she have gone all these days without his touch? She'd wanted him from the beginning, wanted him, wanted him, wanted him…

"Turn your back to me," he whispered.

She did, and he pushed her hair aside and pressed his mouth to the nape of her neck. Her eyes closed; her head fell back as she felt his fingers at the tiny buttons that went from the top of her gown to her waist. He undid them one by one, turning it into an exquisite torment, pausing to kiss each bit of skin as he revealed it.

When he was done, she was trembling.

She began to turn toward him but he stopped her, slid the gown down her arms, lowered his mouth to the delicate juncture of shoulder and throat and pressed his lips there.

She moaned. Whispered his name. Reached back, took his hands, cupped them over her breasts.

Caz groaned as he felt the luscious weight of her breasts in his palms. Slowly he ran his fingers over her nipples, felt them bud and rise at his touch, heard her soft cry of pleasure. She leaned back against him, moved against him, and he slid his hand down to her belly, to the softness between her thighs, pressed her, hard, against his straining erection.

"Megan," he said, his voice low and rough. "Megan…"

She swung around in his arms and he slipped the gown from her shoulders, watching as it pooled at her feet. The gown had been Suliyam; what she wore beneath it was pure, unadulterated twenty-first century seductress, bra and panties of sheerest ivory lace.

"God," he whispered, "you're so beautiful."

Eyes locked to his face, she reached behind her. Undid the bra. Let it fall to her feet.

He felt every muscle in his body tighten with desire. Beautiful? No. The word wasn't enough. His bride was like a dream. Her face. Her eyes. Her mouth.

Her breasts.

They were small. High. The nipples were the deep pink of summer roses, already budding in anticipation of his kiss. A kiss he gave hungrily, bending to her, cupping her breasts,

bringing them to his lips so he could lave the sweet, taut
centers with his tongue and suck them deep into his mouth.

She sobbed out his name as he scooped her into his arms,
carried her to the bed and laid her on it.

"Now," she whispered. Caz, please. I want you now."

She reached for him, ran her hands over his muscled
shoulders, the soft hair on his chest, luxuriated in the race
of his heart under her palms.

"Please," she begged, but when she touched his belt he
caught her hands in one of his, raised them high above her
head.

"Not yet," he said, and watched her face as he cupped
his palm over the bit of lace between her thighs.

Her cry tore through the night, and when he slid his fingers under her panties and found the hot, passion-dampened
flower of her womanhood, she exploded beneath him.

Megan sobbed his name; tears glittered in her eyes but
now he knew they were tears of joy. They were for him,
for what he made her feel, for what was happening to them
both. The realization drove him higher than the mountains,
the moon, the stars. He pulled down the scrap of lace, tore
off his clothes and knelt between her thighs.

"Megan. Look at me."

Her eyes opened and filled with him.

"Who do you belong to?" His voice was a hoarse rasp;
he barely recognized it as his own. "Who?" he demanded,
and she lifted her arms to him.

"You," she whispered. "Only to you, Qasim."

He parted her thighs, touched the engorged tip of his pe-
nis to the soft portal that guarded the entrance to her body,
her heart, her soul. She cried out and arched toward him,
and Caz entered her.

God, oh God.

She was hot and wet and tight. So tight.

He gritted his teeth, forced himself to hold still. He didn't want to hurt her, he didn't want to hurt her, he didn't want to hurt her...

She sighed his name.

"Qasim. Qasim, my husband."

And he was lost.

Groaning, he thrust into her. Filled her. Slid his hands under her bottom and lifted her to him.

"Caz?" she said, her voice a breathless whisper. "Caz. I never knew..."

He drove forward until he was deep inside her. Drove again and again while she sobbed his name and rose to him. And when her body convulsed around him, when she screamed and bit his shoulder, Caz shuddered with a pleasure so intense he thought it might kill him.

But death would have been a small price to pay for what he felt as he fell over the edge of the universe with Megan, with his bride, in his arms.

The moon dipped behind the mountains and still they lay tangled in each other's arms, insulated from reality in their silk cocoon.

At last, Megan stirred. Caz gave her a long, tender kiss and rolled off her. She made a little sound of protest and he kissed her again as he drew her against him. She sighed, settled her head against his chest and laid her arm over his belly.

"I thought you were going to get up," she murmured.

"I'm not going anywhere."

"Um."

He smiled. "That's it?" he said, nuzzling a curl back from her throat and leaving a kiss in its place. "Just, 'um?'"

He felt her lips curve against his damp skin. "Were you hoping for applause, your highness?"

Caz laughed softly. "Well, if you're asking about wedding night traditions..."

Megan nipped at his shoulder. "Don't push your luck, my lord. You'll have to make do with 'um.'" She sighed, stroked her hand over his skin. "That was—"

"Wonderful."

"Yes."

"Amazing."

She smiled. "That, too."

Caz propped his head on his hand, stroked a tangle of soft curls from her face and his smile faded.

"Are you okay?"

"Yes."

"I mean—"

"I know what you mean. And I'm fine."

"You were so tight... I was afraid I'd hurt you."

"No." She caught the tip of his finger between her teeth as he stroked it over her mouth. "I just... I haven't been with anyone in a long time."

Why should that make him feel so happy? "Are the men in California blind?"

She laughed softly. "It's not them, it's me. I've been so focused on my career. You know. College. Grad school. Scrambling up the corporate ladder—"

"Difficult, I'd bet, when some men are busy sawing through the rungs." Megan's surprise showed on her face, and Caz tapped the tip of her nose with his finger. "Now who's being a chauvinist, *kalila?* Don't you think I know that it's tough being a woman in a man's world?"

"Do you, really? I thought—I mean, from the things you said that day in my office..."

"What I said was the truth. Most of my countrymen aren't prepared to see women as equals. Not the ones who live in—what do you call it? The sticks. Not them."

"And you want to change that."

"Yes. Absolutely. I *have* changed it, at least a little, in Suliyam City."

"But not in your palace."

"There, too."

"No way." Megan sat up and pulled the blankets to her chin. "You put me in the harem, remember? There's nothing equal about that."

"That was tradition."

"And that's a clever way of saying one thing and doing another."

"Hey." Caz grabbed her and tugged her down next to him. "Are we going to quarrel?"

Were they? She looked at him and the little sparks of anger that had come to life died away. How could she quarrel with this man now? She was in his arms again, looking up at him, seeing her reflection in his eyes...

And feeling an emotion so overwhelming it terrified her.

"No," she said, on a deep sigh. Smiling, she reached up and pushed his dark hair back from his forehead. "No, we're not going to quarrel."

Caz smiled. "Good. Because there's nothing to quarrel about, *kalila*. The tradition I referred to has to do with the king bringing an unmarried woman to live under his roof."

"Not good, huh?"

"Not good if that same king is about to set off on a tough selling job to a difficult audience."

Megan nodded. "Roads. Schools. Hospitals. All badly needed, and all requiring an infusion of capital."

"Foreign capital, and even the thought of foreign investors having a stake in Suliyam's resources makes some of the old tribal chieftains shudder."

"So, how will you manage?"

"I'll show them facts and figures. They're tough, but they're reasonable."

"Unlike Ahmet."

"Very unlike Ahmet." Caz smiled. "Amazing."

"What?"

"That in all the years I've dealt with financial advisors, accountants and auditors, I never once ended up in bed with one of them."

She laughed. "Not so amazing, considering your last financial wizard was a sixty-year-old man."

Caz tried to look horrified. "You checked up on me?"

"Of course," Megan said primly. "Would T, B and M take on a client without knowing something more about him than you can read in the gossip columns?"

"Damn those columns." Caz rolled onto his belly, bent over her and kissed her mouth. "Half what they print are lies and the other half are exaggerations."

"Ah."

"Ah, what?"

"Ah, no women beating down your doors?"

"No!" He chuckled. "Well, maybe a few."

"No big-spending, easy life?"

"I sowed some wild oats," he admitted.

"Because you could," she teased.

"Because I grew up hearing how I'd some day be king, and the job description didn't sound much like anything a man would want, given half a choice."

The humor had gone out of Caz's voice. He rolled on his back and folded his arms beneath his head.

"Hey," Megan said softly, scooting closer, folding her arms and resting them on his chest. "I was only joking."

"Yeah. I know." He looked at her and smiled. "Would you be shocked if I said being emperor of the universe isn't all it's cracked up to be?"

That was what she'd called him. The memory made her blush, especially now that she'd seen him in action among his people.

"I'd never be shocked at anything you said," she murmured, and brushed her lips against his.

Caz put his arms around her. "No?"

"No."

He cupped the back of her head, brought his mouth to her ear and whispered to her. She caught her breath and drew back.

"See?" he said huskily. "I did shock you, after all."

Megan smiled and gave a catlike stretch so that every inch of her body moved against his.

"On the contrary, my lord. You haven't shocked me. You've fascinated me. I just wonder...can two people really do that?"

Caz felt his body quicken. "Why don't we find out?" he whispered.

He rolled her beneath him. She wrapped her arms around his neck. And by the time they'd answered the question, the room was tinted with the rosy glow of dawn.

They fell asleep, still close in each other's arms, and were awakened by a knock on the door.

"My lord? It is I. Hakim."

Caz sat up and yawned. "What is it?" he called.

"You said you wished to awaken early. It is almost six."

"Six?" Megan whispered in disbelief.

"Hakim's a literalist," Caz whispered back, leaning over and kissing her.

She giggled. Giggled, she thought, and giggled again. Last night, she'd felt as if the world had come to an end and now...

Now, she was so happy it frightened her.

"My lord? I have brought coffee." The doorknob rattled and Megan dived under the blankets. "Shall I—"

"No!" Caz shot from the bed, searched for his trousers and settled for a silk coverlet he wrapped around his waist. "Leave it in the hall."

"But highness..."

"Leave it," Caz said sharply.

"As you wish, sir." Hakim paused. "I've told your pilot to be ready in an hour."

"Yes, yes." Caz glanced at the bed and opened the door just enough to take the tray. "Thank you, Hakim. That's all."

Hakim followed Caz's eyes. "I trust your plans are unchanged, Sheikh Qasim," he said coldly. "That we are, indeed, leaving this place this morning and not lingering for further...festivities."

"Watch yourself," Caz said sharply.

Hakim flushed. "I have only your interests at heart, lord."

Caz elbowed the door shut. "The hell you do," he muttered, and slammed the tray on a table near the bed. After a minute, he sighed and ran his hands through his hair. "Sweetheart? He's gone."

Megan sat up slowly. Her face was pink; the look in her eyes started his anger all over again.

"*Kalila,*" he said, and went to her. "I'm sorry."

She shook her head, pulled back as he tried to embrace her. But Caz was persistent, and the need to be close to him won. Sighing, she put her arms around him and rested her head against his chest.

"Hakim hates me."

"It's not you. It's what you represent. What he sees me doing. All the changes I've made, the changes I intend to make.'' He cupped Megan's shoulders and looked into her eyes. "He served my father."

"And now he serves you."

"That's just the problem, sweetheart. He wants me to be like my father, but I'm not." A muscle knotted in his jaw. "And I don't think he's ever forgiven me for the foreign blood that runs in my veins."

"Foreign...? Oh. Your mother."

"Yeah." A smile curved his lips. "You'd have liked her."

"But she left you."

"She left Suliyam."

"Why? If her husband was here, and her son—"

How did you explain to your American wife that your American mother couldn't handle the heat? The desert? The boundaries set by centuries of tradition?

A few words would have done it, but for some reason he couldn't quite comprehend, Caz didn't want to lay all those things out for Megan's inspection. And that, he knew, was foolish. Megan wasn't really his wife, not by the law of her land. He didn't have to worry about putting ideas in her head. She was going back to her own people, leaving Suliyam...

Leaving him.

The realization stabbed through his heart.

"Come here," he said gruffly, enfolding her in his arms. "Why should we waste time talking about other people?" He bent his head, brushed his mouth over hers. "For now, there's only you and me."

"But Hakim said—"

"Forget Hakim." Caz eased Megan down against the pillows. "Just think about me. About this." He touched his lips to hers, softly, then with growing passion. When he drew back, he knew he couldn't keep the promise he'd made to send her home. He wanted her here, in his arms, in his bed. He wanted to argue with her, laugh with her, share his days and nights with her for as long as fate would permit. "Megan." He took a deep breath. "I know I said I'd send you home as soon as we return to my palace, but..."

"But?"

"But I've been thinking," he said, hurrying the words, refusing to acknowledge the truth of what he felt spreading through his heart. "We still have work to do."

"Work." Her smile faltered. Why had she imagined he might talk about something else? "Yes, of course."

"It's been difficult for you, pretending to have no role in that work."

"Yes." She touched her hand to his cheek. "But I understand, Caz. It's just the way things are here."

"But that would all change, if I could introduce you as my wife."

Megan's heart fluttered. "What are you saying?"

"I know it's asking a great deal, *kalila*. But if you're willing to play the part a little longer..."

She stared into his face, thinking of all the reasons to say no, what he was asking her was out of the question, that it was impossible...

"Kalila." His voice was low and rough with need. "Don't leave me. Not yet."

Their eyes met and held. Then Megan reached for him, brought his mouth down to hers and gave him her answer with her kiss.

CHAPTER ELEVEN

AT NOON, their party left Ahmet's mountain stronghold.

They rode out, Caz on the same black stallion he'd ridden the day they'd arrived. Megan sat sidesaddle before him, secure in the circle of his arm. Ahmet and his men escorted them, whooping and cheering and waving their lances and rifles in the air.

"Tradition," Caz whispered in answer to Megan's inquiring look. "Ahmet honors us. I know it must seem bizarre, but—"

"It seems wonderful. It *is* wonderful." She turned to him and laughed. "The fortress, the horses, the riders…it's perfect."

Caz felt some of the tension drain out of him. All this was strange to his wife. Would she regret that she'd married a man from such an alien culture? It was only temporary, of course, but still, he wanted her to be happy and not judge his people and his country too harshly.

"Do you really like it?"

"Oh, yes! The colors, the sounds… It's magnificent." She laughed again and tilted her head up to his. "Even Ahmet."

Caz grinned. "I'll tell him you said so."

"Don't you dare!"

"What will you offer for my silence?"

Her smile was sweetly wicked. "What would you like?"

He bent his head to hers again and told her. Color flooded her face; heat suffused her body.

"You drive a hard bargain, my lord," she said softly, "but what can I do except agree?"

God, she was wonderful, this wife of his. Caz drew her back more closely against him.

"We have a deal," he said softly. They rode in silence for a few minutes. Then he cleared his throat. "I thought— I was concerned you might find all this…barbaric."

"I guess I might have, not too long ago," she said, with the kind of honesty he'd come to expect from her. "But now—"

"Now?"

"Now, I see things differently."

His lips grazed her temple. "Why, *kalila?*"

The answers were on the tip of her tongue. Because now she rode with a man who was no longer a stranger. Because she was wrapped in the arms of her husband. Because he, and all he represented, were part of her.

Because Qasim had become her life.

"*Kalila.*" Caz spread his hand against her midriff, his thumb just under the rise of her breast. His voice was husky; his breath warmed her face. "Tell me what's changed since we first came here."

Megan turned her face to his. Tell him, she thought, oh, tell him…

A roar went up from the riders as they formed a circle around them. Caz muttered a curse and reined in the stallion. They'd reached the helicopter; Ahmet rode toward them, signaled for silence and began to speak.

Caz bent his head to Megan's, translating softly.

"Ahmet says his timing is lousy."

She laughed. This was far safer ground. "He does, huh?"

"No, but he should." His arms tightened around her.

"Actually, he says I am a lucky man to have won the heart of a woman more beautiful than the moon."

"Translation: He was outmaneuvered."

"Wonderful. The translator needs a translator."

"Am I right?"

"Of course you're right, but we don't have to tell him that. He also says that it's not too late to change my mind. He offers me a hundred horses for you."

"Is that good?"

"It's amazing," Caz said, with a quick smile. "A man can buy twenty excellent wives for one hundred horses. Don't poke your elbow in my ribs, *kalila*. It's the truth. Go on. Smile at our friend. Let him know that you're flattered."

Megan smiled brightly as Caz rattled off a reply.

"What did you tell him?"

"I said he did honor to us both and that it was a tempting offer should I ever—oof!"

"Tempting, indeed."

"Behave yourself, woman. A man doesn't get an offer of one hundred horses every day." Caz drew her more closely against him. "And I told him you were worth a thousand times a hundred horses, *kalila*. I'm a very lucky man."

Megan's heart thudded. She was lucky, too. Caz had changed her life. A week ago, she'd been working in an office, leading a quiet existence. Now, she was the wife of a man who fulfilled every fantasy she'd ever had and some she'd never dared imagine.

She'd almost been foolish enough to tell him so.

She had to remember that none of this was real. He'd made that clear and that was fine, wasn't it? That was exactly the way she wanted things... Wasn't it?

"*Kalila?* What's wrong?"

Everything. Everything was wrong...

"Sweetheart? What's the matter?"

"Nothing," Megan said brightly. "I'm just—I'm a little tired."

"Damn, but I'm a fool! Of course you're tired. I've given you a rough few days." Caz eased her to the ground, then dropped to his feet beside her and swept her into his arms. The crowd gave a throaty roar, but neither of them heard it. "Let's get out of here."

Hakim stepped forward, but the sheikh ignored his aide and carried Megan into the helicopter, settling her into a seat beside him. The 'copter blades began to whirr and the craft lifted, tilted forward and gathered speed until Ahmet and his men were black specks against the towering mountains.

Caz leaned close and put his mouth to Megan's ear. "We'll be home soon."

She nodded and closed her eyes, afraid he might read the truth glittering in them.

Home wasn't a palace by the sea. It wasn't a condo in L.A.

Home was right here, by the side of the man she loved.

Days before, when they'd first arrived at the palace, a handful of men had greeted them. Caz had left her in Hakim's care and driven off with the small delegation.

To a man, no one had acknowledged her presence.

It was all different now.

At least fifty men waited for them in the desert, a long line of Humvees purring behind them like big cats. The men bowed when Caz stepped onto the landing pad, but their dark eyes focused on Megan.

They know, she thought.

What had Caz told them? Had he explained he'd taken her as his wife to save her from Ahmet? Instinct told her they wouldn't understand such a gallant gesture.

But he'd surely told them his marriage was one of convenience?

Then, why were so many of their glances hostile?

Caz greeted them pleasantly. He drew her forward and spoke some more; she heard him use her name. The men looked at her again, then murmured among themselves. Finally, one stepped forward, bowed and began talking, clearly directing his remarks to her.

"He welcomes you," Caz said in a low voice.

Welcomes? She doubted it. She wanted to turn to Caz and burrow into his arms. Instead, she held her head high and smiled.

"Tell him I thank him for coming to greet me."

"He says you have only to ask for whatever you wish and he will scour the earth to find it."

"Tell him I thank him for that, too…and don't mention that I really think he'd like to dab me with honey and tie me to an anthill."

Caz's mouth twitched. "I like the dabbing you with honey part, but only if I can replace the ants with my mouth."

She felt her cheeks color. "Are you sure nobody here understands English?"

"I am positive, and what if they do?" He put his arm around her and drew her against his side. "A man may cherish his own wife."

"Tradition?"

"And one I don't intend to change. Come on, sweetheart. Tell Ari you're grateful for all his good wishes."

"Yes. Of course." She looked at the men, smiled at the one who'd spoken for them all and saw their wary expressions turn to pleasure when she delivered the message in their own language. Caz grinned at her as he led her toward the Humvees.

"You've picked up some of our language," he said. "I'm impressed...though nothing about you should surprise me any more."

"Caz? How did they know about—about us?"

"I sent word," he said as he handed her into the Hummer. "Some of these men are my advisors. It was important that they know of our marriage."

"They think we're really..."

She sounded shocked. Perhaps he should have told her he was going to inform his people that he had married her. Maybe then she wouldn't be staring at him with such a strange expression on her face.

What was she thinking? Moments ago, she'd seemed so happy. Now...

Now, she looked as if she had the weight of the world on her shoulders.

His belly knotted. Was she afraid she might be trapped in a place like this, with a man like him?

"Caz? They really think—"

"Yes." He told himself to smile. "That's not a problem, is it?"

A problem? She wanted to fling herself into his arms. Did this mean he didn't want to treat their marriage as a temporary arrangement? Had he fallen in love with her as she had with him? Did he want her to stay with him, live with him, bear his children and grow old with him?

"No," she said, "of course not. In fact—in fact..."

"In fact what?" he said, trying not to sound as if his life hinged on her answer.

Megan wanted to weep. His tone was polite. That was all. Polite, as if what they were discussing had no real meaning, as if this really were about nothing more important than what he'd told his men.

Caz had married her because he had to, and she couldn't

be fool enough to think that the one night she'd spent in his arms had made him fall in love with her.

"In fact," she said, "you handled it very well."

It? *It?* Their marriage, she meant, and its dissolution. Caz looked at his wife as the Hummer lurched forward. She turned her face to the window.

Apparently the view was more important than him or their marriage.

The warmth of the last minutes, of all the minutes that had slipped by since he'd made her his wife, drained from his heart. He was from one world. She was from another. What they'd shared in the mountains was a fantasy.

What he owed her now was reassurance.

"There's nothing to worry about," he said quietly.

"I'm not—"

"You are. And it's not necessary. We have an agreement. I intend to honor its terms. Why would I do otherwise?"

Why, indeed? Megan's eyes blurred with tears.

"Megan?" Caz touched her shoulder. "I promise you, I'll honor it."

She nodded. He would do what he'd said. He was a good man. An honorable man.

It wasn't his fault he hadn't fallen in love with her.

A week went by, filled with meetings with an endless stream of elders, advisors and chieftains. Of cautious give and take. Of protocol, even when there were times Caz wanted to slam his hand on the table and say, *Can't you see that we need to do these things if we're to survive as a nation?*

But he knew better. He hadn't done anything remotely like that. Instead, he'd listened to questions, provided answers, turned to the woman seated beside him time and time again and always, always, she was ready with a response, a circled paragraph, a list of figures to help him prove his point.

Thanks to Megan, the meetings he'd dreaded had gone well. They'd concluded weeks earlier than he'd expected, and he'd gained the approval he wanted for his proposals.

Even his people were impressed. They'd gone from raising their eyebrows at her presence to looking at her when she spoke. Today, one of his advisors had actually asked her a direct question.

He wondered if she had any idea what an enormous step forward that was, not only for her but also for women in his country. Late this afternoon, the most traditional of the elders had sidled up to him and murmured that perhaps, just perhaps, there was something to be said for educating females.

"Not too much," the old man had added hastily. "Only as much as is necessary for them to be as helpful as your wife, my lord Qasim. She is a gem among women."

Caz, strolling the beach, kicked a small white stone out of his way.

Coming home, he'd imagined what it would be like to show Megan the narrow streets of his city, the ancient bazaars, the hidden places he'd discovered as a boy.

He'd pictured her delight at the little shop that sold silks from China, the half-moon bay just up the coast where dolphins played in the shallows. He'd thought of what it would be like to spend their days exploring his world, their nights making love in the enormous bed that had belonged to five centuries of Suliyam's kings.

Caz bent down, scooped up a shell and tossed it into the sea.

Instead his wife and he were strangers. They were polite to each other. Pleasant. They conferred before the meetings and sometimes after them, but once the day was over, he went his way. She went hers.

And at night...

At night, he lay on the sofa in his sitting room, stared up at the ceiling and tried not to think about Megan lying alone in his bed.

She was only in that bed because he'd commanded it.

"I'll stay in the women's quarters," she'd said the day of their return to the palace.

"The king's wife does not sleep in the women's quarters," he'd said, silently cursing himself for sounding like a stiff-necked martinet. "It would generate talk, and it would not be—"

"Tradition," she'd said, with a taut smile.

Let her think that. The truth was, until his father's marriage to his mother, generations of wives had slept in the women's quarters. It had been the only workable system, back when a king had three, four, a dozen wives, but he'd be damned if he'd tell her that.

It was better than telling her he wanted to know she was in his bed, to be able to dream of her there, with her hair spread over his pillows, even if the image was torture.

How many times had he risen from the sofa, gone to the bedroom door, stood outside it with the blood roaring in his ears as he imagined opening that door, going to her, taking her in his arms and telling her...and telling her...

"Sire?"

Caz swung around. Hakim hurried toward him, huffing and puffing with the effort of walking through the white sand.

"What is it, Hakim? I'm not in the mood to be—"

"It is important, my lord. Your cousin wishes to see you."

"My cousin?"

"Alayna. She has been waiting to meet with you for days."

Hakim spoke the name with all the importance Caz knew it deserved, knew, too, that he had to deal with Alayna eventually. He owed her that...but not now.

"Later, Hakim."

"But Lord Qasim..."

"Later, I said. Tell my cousin that I will see her, but not today."

Hakim nodded stiffly. "Very well, sir. In that case, there is something else. A minor matter..."

"Get to it, man! I told you, I'm not in the mood to be bothered."

"It concerns the woman's departure."

"What woman? What departure?" Caz glowered at his aide. "What are you babbling about?"

"Sir, your pilot will not agree to the flight without your direct permission. I told him there was no need to trouble you, but he insists that—"

"What flight?"

"Miss O'Connell's flight, lord."

"Is this a riddle, Hakim? Her flight to where?"

"To the United States."

Hakim was looking at him as if he were slow-witted. Hell, one of them was.

"Why would Miss O'Connell think she's flying to the States?"

"Because her arrangement with you is at an end, sire."

"What?"

"Is it not so? The woman says—"

"You didn't think it necessary to speak with me?"

"I was only trying to save you the bother, lord. The woman—"

Caz took a step forward, his fists bunched at his sides.

"The woman," he said, his voice low and menacing, "is my wife. The Sheikha. You will refer to her by title. Is that clear?"

"But my lord…"

"Is it clear, damn you?"

He watched his aide's face whiten.

"Yes, lord. Of course. Forgive me, sir."

But Caz wasn't listening. He'd already started running toward the palace.

Megan had almost finished packing when the door burst open.

"What in hell are you doing?"

His voice roared through the room. He was angry, but she'd expected that. She'd expected him to confront her, too. Hakim had been happy to make the arrangements for her departure without involving Caz—the aide made no pretence of how eager he was to see her gone—but she'd suspected it wouldn't be possible.

Nothing happened in this antiquated corner of the world without the involvement of Sheikh Qasim, and she'd known he would not take kindly to letting her leave without some sort of confrontation.

All week, she'd sensed that his behavior—polite, formal, distant—masked a growing anger. And what in hell did *he* have to be angry about? She was the same woman she'd always been; Caz was the one who'd changed. One moment he'd been her passionate lover, the next he'd become…

There was no way to describe what he'd become. Cold, uncaring, disinterested. All that, and more.

And it hurt.

Still, she wasn't prepared for the rage flashing in his eyes. Well, she thought, taking a blouse from its hanger, that was fine.

She'd rather deal with his anger than with his disinterest. Better to go toe-to-toe with him than to lie in his bed, alone and unhappy, crying herself to sleep, and wasn't that a stupid thing to have done all these nights? What was there to cry about? She'd figured out, days ago, that she'd never really fallen in love with Caz. Pretty pathetic, when a modern woman had to feed herself a lie about love rather than admit all she'd wanted was to sleep with a man.

"Did you hear me? I said—"

"I heard you. What does it look like I'm doing?" Megan folded the blouse neatly. Damn, her hands were shaking. "I'm packing."

"The hell you are!"

She told herself to keep calm. He was trying to upset her, and she'd be damned if she'd let him succeed.

"Packing is generally the first step before a person leaves," she said calmly.

"Perhaps you've forgotten that you work for me."

"Perhaps *you've* forgotten that my job here is done."

"It's done when I say it is."

"It's done when the meetings end. Well, they ended."

"There's also the little matter of our marriage."

She looked up. His eyes were so narrow she could hardly see them and a muscle beat rapidly in his jaw. Dark and dangerous, indeed. How about dark, dangerous and insufferable? How kind of him to remind her of some of the things she hadn't liked about him when they met.

"There is no marriage, remember? Not a real one."

"Would you say that if we'd been married in Los Angeles?"

"We *weren't* married in Los Angeles, we were married in Suliyam, and you made it perfectly clear that—"

"Are you suggesting marriages here are not legal?"

"I'm simply reminding you of what you told me. This marriage isn't binding."

Caz folded his arms and glowered. She was right. That was what he'd told her. What was wrong with him? Why was he so damned angry?

And why did the statement about their marriage sound so different, coming from her?

Because he was the king, that was why. If anyone ended this union, it would be him.

He told her that, and when she barked a laugh, he felt the heat rise to his face.

"Just listen to yourself, Qasim. You are unbelievab—"

"I am your husband," he roared. "And in Suliyam, a wife may not leave her husband without permission."

"Is that what this is all about? You want me to grovel? Well, I won't. You told me I would be free to leave, that our vows had no meaning, that—"

Caz caught her by the shoulders and lifted her to her toes. "I said the marriage would have no meaning, that I would annul it, that you would have to do nothing once you were back in the States…but you're still in my country. Until I choose to set you free, you belong to me."

Damn it, he thought in disgust, was he really calling up one of the barbaric traditions he'd sought to destroy? From the way his wife was looking at him, he sure as hell was, but what was he supposed to do? Let a woman play him for a fool? Let a woman take the upper hand?

Let this woman, only this woman, steal his heart and walk out of his life?

Didn't she feel anything for him? She did. She had to. He remembered that long night she'd spent in his arms. How she'd sighed, moved, whispered his name, and suddenly nothing mattered but wiping away the deceit they'd woven and facing the truth.

"Megan," he said hoarsely, and when she looked into his eyes, he gathered her against him and kissed her.

She fought him. Struggled to tear her mouth from his. He didn't have the words to tell her what she meant to him, but he could show her. He could kiss her until she knew his hunger, until she responded as she had on their wedding night.

And then, when he'd almost lost hope, her mouth softened. Clung to his. She made a little sound that was as much despair as it was surrender. It almost broke his heart when he tasted the salt of her tears on her lips.

"*Kalila*. Don't cry."

She shook her head. "Caz. I beg you. Let me go."

"I don't want you to leave me."

"Yes, you do. Whatever was between us died when we came back here. That time in the mountains was an illusion."

"It was real," he said fiercely. She wouldn't look at him and he hunched down, cupped her face, forced her to meet his eyes. "I love you."

The words were true. He knew it as soon as he spoke them.

"I beg you, *kalila*. Don't leave me. Stay with me. Be my wife. Lie in my arms at night, stay by my side during the day. I love you, Megan. I love—"

Megan sobbed his name, brought his face down to hers and gave her husband the answer he sought in her kiss.

CHAPTER TWELVE

MEGAN awoke lying curled against her husband, her head on his chest, her hand spread over his heart.

Doves cooed to each other in the courtyard beneath the bedroom window; she could hear the sea beating gently against the crescent of white sand beach only a short distance away.

Caz, still asleep, lay on his back. With just a little effort, she could look up and see his firm chin, his softly stubbled jaw.

How she loved him! How she loved waking like this each morning, lying close to him, feeling the glorious weight of his arm wrapped around her

Two weeks ago, she'd probably have described the way he held her as possessive. Now, she thought of it as protective.

Amazing, how her perspective had changed in fourteen short days.

Sometimes, lying in his embrace, she wondered if other married people were this happy. It didn't seem possible. To begin each day with so much joy in your heart and end it thanking whatever gods might be listening for the miracle that had brought such love into your life?

Nobody else could feel this way. Nobody. Not even her brothers. Not even her sister. Keir and Cullen might look at their wives with their hearts shining in their eyes; Fallon's smile might turn soft and dreamy when Stefano entered the room, but could any of them really know such bliss?

Impossible.

Surely she was the only woman in the world who loved a man so deeply. Absolutely, she was the only one loved so deeply in return. Caz was—he was—

"Beautiful," Caz murmured in a voice husky with sleep.

Megan smiled as her husband rolled her onto her back. "Good morning," she said softly.

He smiled, too, and brushed his lips over hers. "Good morning, *kalila*. When was the last time I told you that I love you?"

"Well, let's see..." Megan linked her hands behind his neck. "Was it at dinner? Maybe it was when we came to bed. It might have been later than that, when we decided to go down to the beach to try to count the stars."

"Mmm." Caz nuzzled a tangle of auburn curls from her shoulder and nipped lightly at the tender flesh he'd exposed. "You forgot early this morning. I woke you at dawn, remember?"

Indeed, he had. Her skin still tingled at the memory. "Did you?" She batted her lashes. "I don't remember that, my Lord."

"You don't, huh?"

"No. You might have to remind—" She caught her breath as he kissed her breast, teased the nipple with tongue and teeth, then sucked it into his mouth. "Yes. Oh, yes, I remember you did that."

He slid down her body, kissing her belly, nuzzling apart her thighs, burying his face in the heat of her, the scent of her, the essence of this woman who had changed his life.

"Do you remember this, too?" he whispered, slipping his hands beneath her, lifting her to his mouth, opening her to him so he could taste her, feast on her, luxuriate in the soft moans that drove him crazy.

"Caz. Caz…"

"Tell me," he said thickly. "Say the words, *kalila*. I need to hear them."

"I love you," Megan whispered, "love you, love you, love…"

She cried out and he rose above her, sheathed himself in her, and when she cried out again, he fell with her into that heart-stopping moment in time when they were alone in the endless universe.

"Megan?"

"Mmm."

Caz propped himself on his elbow, smiled as he traced the tip of his finger down her nose, over her lips and down her chin.

"Come on, *kalila*. Stay awake. I have something important to discuss with you."

"What does that mean?"

"It means, I want you to pay attention."

"No." She rolled on her belly, pushed him back against the pillows and folded her arms on his chest. "Ka-lee-lah. What's it mean?"

"You don't know?"

"Uh uh. I've meant to ask you endless times."

"You've picked up so much of my language…" He grinned. "But then, I don't suppose any of the men we've met with address each other as 'sweetheart.'"

"Sweetheart?" He nodded; she smiled. "It has a lovely sound."

"I'm glad you approve."

Megan nipped his bottom lip. "Don't take that smart-alecky tone with me, Lord Qasim."

"Smart what?"

"You understand what I said. You're as American as I am."

"No, I'm not."

"You are."

He smiled. After a few seconds, he cleared his throat. "Megan? Do you miss America very much?"

"A little," she said, with the honesty he loved. "But I have you, and you mean more to me than anything else."

Caz pressed a kiss into her hair. "I promise, we'll go back for a visit very soon."

"And I'll introduce you to my family." Megan's smile faltered. "I'm not looking forward to that. Oh," she said quickly, "I didn't mean that the way it sounded. I only meant… They'll be hurt, that I didn't tell them we were getting married."

"Well, we'll explain that we didn't know about it until it happened—unless you don't want them to hear that part."

"That you married me to save me from the big, bad wolf?" She laughed. "Of course I want them to hear it. They'll love it. My brothers will take you straight into the O'Connell clan because you're so macho, and my sisters will ooh and ahh. It's not every modern-day woman finds her own knight in shining armor." Megan tucked a fingertip into a soft curl on his chest. "I guess what'll upset them is that they weren't part of our wedding. Well, I'll just point out that they couldn't have been."

"No," Caz said wryly, "not with Ahmet standing in for best man."

"And maid of honor." Megan giggled. "There's a thought. Ahmet, in a bridesmaid's gown. Can't you just see it?"

"What I can see," Caz said, getting up and scooping her

into his arms, "is you in white lace, me in a tux, your sisters—how many are there?"

"Two," she answered, puzzled, "but—"

"Two sisters in pink or yellow or whatever you like best, and those three brothers-in-law of mine in tuxes." He grinned as he carried her into the adjoining bathroom and set her on her feet next to the step-up marble tub. "If I have to wear a monkey suit, so do they."

"I'm sure they'll love you to pieces for your kindness, but what are you talking about?"

"Our wedding, *kalila*. What else would impel a sane man into wearing a tuxedo?"

"We've already had our wedding."

"Not a real one, sweetheart." Caz turned on the water and gathered her into his arms as it thundered into the enormous tub. "You deserve the kind of wedding girls dream of."

Megan leaned back in his arms. "What do you know of wedding dreams, Lord Qasim?"

"I know," Caz said with a lift of his eyebrows. "I'm at an age where I've been to enough weddings to know that it certainly isn't the grooms who want the tuxedos, the engraved invitations, the fiftieth microwave oven that you have to pretend is the first you've received."

"Just goes to show you've been going to the wrong parties. My relatives will know enough to give us a gift certificate for a day spent skydiving."

Caz raised his eyebrows. "Don't tell me. My wife skydives?"

"She does," Megan said primly. "And she's never found anything she enjoys more."

"She hasn't, huh?"

A smile curled across her lips. "Well," she said softly, "not until now." Caz kissed her and she leaned back in his arms and sighed. "You poor man. All those weddings, and I bet you never figured you'd go to one of your own."

Something changed in his expression. A shift of his smile, a darkening of his eyes…she wasn't sure what, but she knew she'd seen something.

"Caz? What's the matter?"

"Nothing."

"Tell me. You looked—"

"I looked like a man contemplating an incredible reality, sweetheart." He cupped her face, threaded his fingers into her hair. "I love you, with all my heart."

"That's good. It's very, very good because I love you, too."

"I want to make you my wife again, this time in a white wedding with your whole family present. Your mother. Your father."

"My stepfather." She kissed his mouth. "Amazing, isn't it, that there are still things we don't know about each other?"

"There's plenty of time to learn."

"Yes. There is. A lifetime." She smiled. "Where will we hold this wedding?"

"Here. In the palace. Unless you'd rather—"

"I love the idea. So will my sisters. And my sisters-in-law." A mischievous grin lit her face. "And my brothers, and my brother-in-law, and a bunch of fat, gorgeous babies. The O'Connells are a big clan, Sheikh Qasim, and growing."

"I hope so," Caz said, and spread his hand over her belly. "I want children, *kalila*. Little girls, with your beautiful eyes."

"Sons, with your wonderful smile." Her voice broke. "Caz, I'm so happy."

"Yes," he whispered, "yes, I know, *kalila*. I know."

He kissed her, kissed her again as he stepped into the huge marble tub with her in his arms, and soon the only sounds in the room were the soft splash of water, whispers and sighs.

Megan checked the time, tried to figure out the corresponding hour in New York, Boston, Sicily, Connecticut and Las Vegas, and gave up.

So what if she woke everybody? She was remiss as it was; she should have phoned home days ago to tell her family about Caz, but these new things—that she was bringing her husband home to meet them soon, that they'd all be attending a wedding in Suliyam—couldn't wait.

She called Bree first and reached her sister's voice mail.

"Aren't you ever home?" she demanded. "Honestly, Briana, how can I tell you my news if you're not there?"

Then she disconnected. It was a wicked thing to do, but Bree deserved it.

Keir and Cassie were next. *Hello,* Keir's voice said, *you've reached the O'Connells. We can't take your call right now...*

"For heaven's sake," Megan grumbled, and dialed again.

Fallon and Stefano weren't home, either. Their housekeeper answered, but since Megan's knowledge of Italian and the housekeeper's knowledge of English just about totaled zero, she didn't get much further than, "Just tell them Megan called."

Sean's cell phone didn't answer at all, and when she tried to reach Cullen and Marissa, all she got was static.

Megan hit the disconnect button and rolled her eyes. Great. She had the most wonderful news of her life and nobody to share it with.

Well, no. Her mother was probably reachable in Las Vegas, but she wanted to tell the others first. Ma would start making plans, and she preferred the plans she'd just made with Caz. Life would be simpler if she had the backing of Fallon and Briana.

And wasn't that silly?

Her mother would be thrilled for her. *Aren't you ever going to meet a man and fall in love, Megan?* Mary was always saying. She'd been saying it more often lately, at least once at each O'Connell wedding.

Megan smiled, picked up the phone...

"Miss O'Connell?"

It was Hakim. So much for ET calling home, Megan thought, and tossed the phone aside.

"Yes, Hakim. What is it?"

"Will you please come with me?"

He was supposed to address her as "my lady." She'd heard Caz tell him that. It was what everyone called her, even though she'd told her husband she'd be happy if they just called her Megan.

"'My lady' is traditional," he'd replied, and softened the starchy answer with a quick grin. "Trust me, sweetheart. If I told my people to address you by your first name, they'd die of shock."

So she was "my lady" to her husband's people, even to Hakim...except when Caz wasn't there. She hadn't made an issue of it. Her husband's aide had unresolved issues with all that had happened. He also made her uncomfortable as hell, but she hadn't told Caz that, either.

Hakim would come around.

"Come with you where?" she asked politely. "Has my husband sent for me?"

"Your husband is busy, Miss O'Connell. That is why I've come for you."

Megan nodded. Caz had some sort of meeting this afternoon. "Will you need me with you?" she'd asked, and he'd said no, not today.

"Tired of having me around already," she teased, and he'd caught her in his arms and gathered her close.

"Never," he'd told her, his eyes so serious, his tone so defiant, that she'd slipped her arms around him and kissed him.

Well, something must have changed, she thought as she followed Hakim down the wide hall that led to the formal meeting rooms of the palace. Perhaps she should have brought her briefcase. Her notes.

"Hakim. Wait a minute. Who's my husband meeting with? I'd like to go back to our rooms and get my papers."

Hakim made an abrupt right. They'd entered a narrow corridor, one she'd never seen before.

"Hakim? I said—"

The aide made another sharp right. A latticework door loomed ahead.

"You will not need your papers for this, Miss O'Connell."

His voice had dropped to a whisper that made the hair rise on the back of her neck.

"What is this?" she said sharply. "Where is my husband?"

"He is there, beyond that door."

Hakim pressed his back to the wall and motioned her past him. Megan stared at the cold eyes, the slash of a mouth. She didn't want to move…

Motion through the lattice caught her eye.

She saw her husband, standing in the center of a small room. A woman was with him.

Her heart filled with dread. *Don't look,* a voice inside her whispered. *Megan, don't look…*

Her feet moved forward, seemingly of their own volition.

She put her eye to the lattice, stared at the woman…and immediately recognized her. This was who she'd seen with Caz weeks ago, the stunning brunette who'd kissed him.

His cousin, Caz had said. She'd kissed him to thank him for not forcing her to marry a man she didn't love.

She wasn't kissing him now. Instead she was wrapped in his arms, her eyes closed, her face pressed to his chest. Caz…Caz's eyes were closed, too. His chin rested on the top of the woman's head.

A pulse began beating in Megan's temple. She swung around, brushed past Hakim and hurried down the hall.

"Miss O'Connell! Wait."

"I'm not going to spy on my husband."

Hakim caught up to her where the corridor made its turn. "You are my lord's wife. There are things you must know."

Megan spun toward him. "I *do* know! Do you think you can make me jealous? My husband told me of this woman. She is his cousin."

"Yes, that is correct."

"She was to marry a man she didn't love."

Hakim inclined his head. "That is correct, too."

"She loves another man. My husband arranged for her to be with that man."

"He did."

"And—and what we just saw…" Megan drew a shuddering breath. "What we saw was—it was just her, thanking my husband again."

"You are right, Miss O'Connell. It is all as you say."

"Then what is this all about? Why did you bring me here? Why did you want me to see this?"

"You are not one of us."

"Well, that's an amazing revelation!"

"You know nothing of our traditions."

"Oh, for God's sake—"

She started to turn away. Hakim caught her arm. It was, she knew, as close to a capital offense as one could come in Suliyam. She was not just a woman, she was the king's wife.

Her heart beat faster. She was alone in a place that looked as if no one even knew it existed, and the man with her had hated her from the minute he'd set eyes on her.

"Take your hands off me," she said sharply, "or my husband will hear of this."

"You have bewitched him, " Hakim said, his words thick with disdain.

"Did you hear me? Let go!"

"He thinks he loves you."

"He does love me. And I love him. Now, take your hand away."

"Love." Hakim spat out the word. "What does it mean?"

"Everything, but you wouldn't understand that."

"Love is a western fantasy. What we have believe in here is—"

"Tradition? As in, marrying off the sheikh's cousin to a man she doesn't love? The only thing that can come of such a tradition is the pain of a broken heart."

Hakim stepped toward her. Megan almost shrank back against the wall. She'd never seen such hatred in anyone's face.

"The woman is called Alayna. She was betrothed."

"Yes, to a man she didn't love. It's fascinating, but it has nothing to do with me."

"At first, when she came to my lord Qasim to beg his mercy, he denied her. He understood the meaning of tradition."

"But he's changed. Is that why you hate me, Hakim? Because you think I'm responsible for that?"

"When she came to him again, you had arrived in the palace." Hakim's mouth twisted. "Again, she pleaded for my lord's understanding. And that time, he said he would find a way to help her."

"Does it trouble you to know that your king has a heart?"

"Does it trouble you to know you are interfering in our way of life?"

"That's not true."

"You married Lord Qasim."

"I did. And I'm going to marry him again. Are you so blind that you can't understand the world is changing? Just because I'm a foreigner—"

"Our king is already betrothed!"

Megan stared at Hakim. "What?"

"To Alayna. They were pledged to each other at birth."

What had she said to Caz, just this morning? *There are things we don't know about each other...* And he'd smiled and said they had their whole lives to learn those things...

"A betrothal isn't a marriage," Megan said. Her voice shook, and she cleared her throat. "Obviously my husband changed his mind. He married me, not Alayna."

"He married you, and said he would divorce you. But he didn't. You ensnared him."

"I'm not listening to another moment of this non—"

"Alayna's people will not tolerate such an insult. They will not permit her to be disgraced."

"Don't you get it? Alayna didn't want to go through with this marriage. She won't be disgraced, she'll be thrilled! Her family will understand, once she explains it to them."

Hakim's face grew dark. "You are a fool, Miss O'Connell! Alayna will not be able to hold up her head. Her family will have to do something about what Lord Qasim has done, or she will never find another husband."

"Even if that's true, I'm not responsible for it. You said

yourself, my husband has already promised to help Alayna.''

''Only after he met you. After you bewitched him, and then married him and refused to divorce him.''

''Listen to me, old man. My husband doesn't want a divorce. He wants—''

''You. Yes. And to get you, he will bring dishonor to a foolish girl, to an important family, to an entire people.''

''No. No, I don't believe you.'' Megan gave an unsteady laugh. ''You make it sound as if I'm going to—to bring down the throne!''

''You well may,'' Hakim said grimly. ''At the very least, you will make it impossible for Lord Qasim to implement the changes he's worked so hard to achieve.''

''You're wrong,'' Megan said desperately. ''I've been in all those meetings. My husband's ideas have been well-received.''

''Your husband has had a difficult enough time convincing his people to follow his new ways. Now he stands to lose the respect of an entire faction. He's flaunted the centuries-old traditions that govern who he is to marry, who is to sit beside him as queen, who will provide him with heirs to the throne.''

''Lies, all of it! Qasim's father married a foreigner, too.''

''Only after his first wife died.'' Hakim leaned toward her so that she felt his hot breath on her face. ''You have put the sheikh in great danger.''

''Danger?'' Megan felt her knees turn watery. ''How—how can he be in danger?''

''We are a people of ancient traditions. The only way to assuage the stain of dishonor is with blood.''

''No.'' She shook her head. ''I don't believe that. Qasim has changed things here.''

"Traditions are not changed as easily as plans for roads and hospitals."

"I'll speak with him. I'll ask him if—"

"What will you ask him? Or rather, what will he tell you? Do you think he'll let you know what he risks for you?" Hakim's eyes bored into hers. "You say you love the sheikh. Perhaps you do. Then I must ask... Do you love him enough to give him up, or will you wait until he loses his throne, his kingdom, his people...his life?"

Hours later, an eternity later, Megan lay beside Caz in their bed.

The night was silent and dark, heavy with moisture from a storm that was rolling in over the sea.

She knew what she had to do, and that she should have done it by now, but she'd wanted one more night, one more memory to warm her through the years that stretched ahead.

Caz had made love to her.

She had made love to him.

For the last time, her heart kept saying, for the last time.

Each kiss, each caress had been filled with the pain of what she knew would come next. And it was time to do it. Now, before she lost her courage.

But first—first, one last kiss...

Megan brushed her lips over her those of her sleeping husband. His mouth softened, clung to hers, and she almost let herself sink into the kiss.

But she didn't.

She slid from under his arm, rolled to the edge of the bed and reached for the robe she'd deliberately left within reach earlier in the evening. Once she had it on, sash firmly tied, she rose to her feet.

"Caz?"

Caz sighed and rolled on his belly.

"Caz, wake up. I want to talk to you."

"Mmm." He turned over and looked at her. A little smile tugged at the corner of his mouth. "What are you doing, *kalila?* Come back here," he said, holding out his hand. "It's the middle of the night."

"We have to talk."

"Can't you sleep?" His smile turned soft and sexy. "I'll bet I can think of a way to make you relax."

She looked at him. At his beloved face. Her legs were threatening to give way; she wanted to sit down before they did, but sitting near him would be the end of her resolve.

"I phoned my family, Caz. To tell them about us.

His eyes locked on hers. "And?"

"And—and…"

"And, they don't approve."

He saw the surprise on her face, but her family's concern was nothing less than he'd expected. If he had a daughter—and he would, someday, a perfect, beautiful image of his wife—if he had a daughter and she announced she'd married a man they'd never met, a man who was king of a country in the middle of nowhere, he wouldn't approve, either. Hell, he'd probably go crazy!

"No. They'd don't."

He sat up against the pillows, the silk blanket draping just below his navel. "Megan. Listen to me—"

"They—they raised a lot of valid issues."

"Valid issues?" he said, his voice suddenly soft as smoke.

"Yes. They asked me to think about what it would be like for me to live here instead of in America. To live here with—with someone so different from me."

"Who is 'they?'" His tone was flat. "Did you discuss Suliyam and me with your entire family?"

"No. Actually—actually, I only talked to Sean," she said,

plucking her brother's name out of the air. "But he gave me the same advice they'd all give me, I'm sure."

"And that advice was?"

"That I go home. Think things over."

Caz said nothing for a long minute. Then he threw off the blanket, reached for his trousers and pulled them on.

"Let's cut to the bottom line. You're going home, and you're not coming back. Am I right?"

Tears stung her eyes but she knew she mustn't let him see them.

"Megan? Am I right? Are you leaving me?"

No. Oh, no. How can I leave you, my love? How can I live without you...

"Yes," she said. "I am."

She hadn't known what to expect after she told him. Whatever it was, it hadn't been this. The stony face. The empty eyes. The terrible, awful stillness.

"I wish—I wish it could be different, but—"

"I don't."

She stiffened. "You don't?"

"No." He walked around the bed and she took an instinctive step back, but he went past her to the dressing room. "Actually it's a relief." His voice grew muffled; he came back into the bedroom tugging a black sweater over his head. "I let things get away from me when I suggested marriage. You're right. It wouldn't have worked. We have nothing in common, except in bed."

His words stung. Was he saving face, or was he telling her the truth? It didn't matter. This was the way things had to end. She'd known it, in her heart, from the minute he'd taken her to bed on their wedding night.

"I want you to know..." Her voice trembled and she began again. "I—I enjoyed our time together. It was—it was—"

"Yes," he said coldly. "It was."

Caz reached for the phone and pressed a button.

"Hakim? Have my plane readied. Yes, now. Miss O'Connell will be flying to the States. Have someone come for her." He hung up and turned back to Megan. "I really think it's best that you leave right away, Megan. I'm sure your brother would prefer to have you back among civilized people as soon as possible."

He started to the door. Megan took a step. "Caz? Caz, please. Don't—don't walk away from me. I want to—I want to—"

"What do you want?" He swung toward her, and now, at last, she could see the rage in his face. "A final roll between the sheets? Another reminder of what it's like to lie in the arms of a barbarian?"

"That's cruel! I never—"

"Perhaps my assurance that I won't try to claim our marriage is valid." He came toward her, his eyes the color of slate after a winter storm, and she stumbled back against the wall. "Believe me, I won't. Did I mention that our marriage could be dissolved, just like that?" He snapped his fingers an inch from her face. "It's one of the perks of being a man in my country. If a husband doesn't want his wife, all he has to do it tell her so." Caz's lips pulled back from his teeth. "I don't want you for my wife anymore, Megan O'Connell. I divorce you."

"You mean, all along, any time, you could have—"

"Anytime at all," he said smugly.

Why should that shock her? And yet, it did. The easily spoken words, the realization that she'd been little more than a toy, filled her with rage.

"Bastard," she hissed, and slammed her hand against his face.

He caught her wrist, twisted it hard enough so she gasped.

"Go back where you belong, Megan O'Connell. Where life is safe and sanitized, where nothing can touch you." He yanked her forward, crushed her mouth beneath his. She tasted him, tasted salt, tasted blood...

And then he was gone and she was alone, and the lifetime she'd lived in a few short weeks was little more than a dream.

CHAPTER THIRTEEN

BRIANA O'CONNELL leaned into her sister's refrigerator, surveyed the shelves and muttered an unladylike word under her breath.

"Honestly, Meg, there's nothing to eat in this thing!"

Megan, sitting on the living room sofa, hunched farther over the employment section of the Sunday Times and circled an ad with her pen.

"Unless you think cottage cheese is edible. Or yogurt."

Megan turned the page, circled another ad, then crossed t out.

"And what, pray tell, is this green thing? Yuck!"

Only one column of advertisements left and only one decent prospect so far. Just her luck, to be job-hunting when the economy was heading south.

"Megan," Bree said, slamming the fridge door closed, "I love you with all my heart, sweetie, but your taste in food leaves something to be desired. Do you hear me?"

"The entire city of Los Angeles hears you," Megan grumbled. "Order a pizza."

"Good idea." Bree yanked the takeout pizza menu from under the magnet that held it to the fridge and strolled into the living room. "How's this sound? An extra large with garlic, olives, onions, bacon, anchovies, sausage..."

Megan looked up. Bree grinned.

"Figured that would get your attention." Her voice softened. "Come on, sis. Put the paper away and let's go out for something to eat."

"I'm really not—"

"Hungry. Yes, I know." Bree plopped down on a chair opposite the sofa. "Well, who would be, considering the choice of yummy things in your refrigerator?"

"I haven't been paying much attention to what I buy lately. You want anchovies and bacon? Go ahead. Order it."

"Not even I'm that nuts." Briana sat back. She crossed her legs, bounced one foot up and down, then cleared her throat. "So, how's the big job hunt going? Anything good today?"

Megan sighed, tossed her pen aside and looked at Briana. "No."

"Nobody wants accountants in L.A.?"

"They want bookkeepers who think they're accountants, and accountants willing to be paid like bookkeepers."

"Which means?"

"Which means, I'm overqualified."

"How about trying a headhunter? Don't you need to go through a lot of mumbo-jumbo to find the really good listings?"

"I'm listed with somebody."

"Nothing, huh?"

"Nope." Megan stood up. "How about if I phone in the pizza order?"

"Fine. Just make sure you don't ask for bacon. Or anchovies. Or—"

"Sausage," Megan said, and grinned. "Don't worry. I'm not nuts, either."

Briana smiled back at her. Then she rose, too, unlocked the door for the pizza guy, and followed Megan into the kitchen.

"How about that economics degree of yours?" she said,

after Megan had phoned in their order. "Why not look for a job in that field?"

"I told you the reason."

"No, you didn't," Bree said, opening the fridge and taking out a container of orange juice.

"Yes, I did."

"You said the turkey at Tremont, Burnside and Macomb would never give you a decent reference."

"See? I did tell you."

"You said he wouldn't. You didn't said *why* he wouldn't." Bree opened the OJ and took a sniff. "I always thought you were good at your work."

"I am."

"But?"

"But…" Megan hesitated. "But, I sort of quit in the middle of an assignment."

"Whoa. Doesn't sound like you." Bree sniffed the juice again. "This stuff smells funky."

Megan rolled her eyes, grabbed the container and dumped the contents into the sink. "You should have told me you were coming, Bree. I'd have had time to shop."

"I didn't know I was coming, remember? I'd have to be psychic to know they were gonna ground all planes west of the Rockies because of bad weather in Colorado." Briana pushed out her bottom lip. "You want, I'll go to a hotel…"

"No!" Megan grabbed her sister and hugged her tight. "Of course I don't want that, Sis. I'm just—" She drew back. "I'm edgy, that's all."

"Yeah," Bree said wryly, "I noticed." She leaned back against the sink and folded her arms. "So, why'd you quit?"

"Huh? Oh. Oh, well, I—I just did."

"Try again."

"I, um, I wasn't getting along with the client. And, uh, and I decided it was in everyone's best interest if I just—"

"Remember when we were kids? And I sort of borrowed one of Fallon's skirts? And she'd told me a zillion times to stay out of her closet?"

"Bree. Whatever you're trying to say—"

"I burned a hole in it. Well, Donny Hucksacker burned a hole in it, trying to show how grown up he was by smoking a cigarette, except he dropped it and... Okay, okay, I'll get to the point. I was terrified of letting Fallon know what I'd done, and you took pity on me and said you'd take the blame, and you tried to but it didn't work because she took one look at your face and—"

"Oh, for heaven's sake! Where are you going with this?"

"I'm just pointing out that you are the world's worst liar. Whatever happened with you and that client was a lot more than not getting along."

Megan stared at her sister. "Aren't you supposed to phone the airline every hour?"

"I called them twenty minutes ago."

"Right. Well—well, I just remembered, I have an appointment with that headhunter."

"On Sunday?" Bree smiled sweetly. "I don't think so."

"Look here, Briana—"

"Look here, yourself, Megan Nicole O'Connell! When are you going to tell me what's going on, huh? A month ago, you left this cryptic message on my answering machine—"

"There was nothing cryptic about it."

"Oh, give me a break." Bree raised her eyebrows as well as her voice. "'Hi, this is Megan. I'm leaving for a place you never heard of and coming back who knows when, and, be still my heart, I'll be working with a guy who's absolutely D and D...'"

"I never said that!"

Briana flashed a triumphant smile. "You didn't have to.

You went to Suliyam, and your client was Sheikh Qasim Something-or-Other, and me oh my, if he isn't Dark and Dangerous, nobody is.''

Megan slapped her hands on her hips. "How do you know all that?"

"It was in one of those business magazines, an article about him working with a consultant from T, B and M. And there was a picture of the guy and after I wiped the drool off my chin I said to myself, 'Self, big sister Megan is off in the wilds with a stud.'" Briana slapped her hands on her hips, too. "And before you say, 'You? Reading a business magazine,' the answer is yes, me, reading a business magazine. I was at the dentist's and all the *Cosmo*s and *Elle*s were gone."

"Now who's the liar?"

"Don't try and change the subject. Is he?"

Megan sighed. The right answer was, "Is he what?" But she'd only be delaying things. Her sister could be as persistent as a dog with a bone.

"Yes. He is. D and D to the core."

"I knew it!"

"So what? Being dark and dangerous isn't everything."

"Oh."

The "oh" was filled with meaning. Megan refused to take the bait. Instead she yanked open a cupboard and took out two plates.

"Here. Make yourself useful. Set the table so that we can eat as soon as the pizza gets here."

"Something happened," Bree said. "Between you and the sheikh."

"I told you what happened," Megan said, bustling around the kitchen as if it were the size of a skating rink instead of a closet. "We didn't get along. For heaven's sake, are you just going to stand there? Take these napkins. Take extras. Take—''

''You and he had a thing going.''

Megan looked at her sister. ''Give it up,'' she said quietly.

''I'm right! You got it on with the sheikh!''

''Such an adult turn of phrase,'' Megan said coldly.

Bree batted her lashes. ''Was he good?''

''I am not going to discuss Caz with you.''

''Caz, huh?''

''You're wasting your time.''

''I am?''

''Yes. What happened in Suliyam happened. It didn't mean a thing. I've stopped thinking about it, and I'm not interested in talking about it.'' Megan's voice trembled and she glared at her sister. ''You hear me, Briana? I am not going to talk about this,'' she said, and burst into tears.

''Oh, baby!'' Briana hurried to her sister's side and wrapped an arm around her shoulders. ''Honey, I'm so sorry! I was just teasing, you know? I never expected…''

''No. Neither did—neither did—''

Megan buried her face in her hands and wept. She hadn't cried, not once since she'd left Caz. She'd been all business when she got home, picking up her mail from Mrs. Hansen across the way, going to work the next day, calmly telling The Worm that she'd be happy to bring someone else up to speed on the Suliyam assignment but that she was sorry, she'd have to sign off.

The Worm, as she'd anticipated, was overjoyed.

''In that case,'' he'd said, all but rubbing his hands, ''you're fired.''

She'd anticipated that, too.

The only thing she hadn't anticipated was the yawning emptiness in her heart, the questions that raced through her

head like a cat chasing its own tail. Was it true? Had Caz
been planning on putting her out of his life, or had he only
said those terrible things because she'd wounded him? She
told herself it didn't matter, that what counted was that she'd
left him, left Suliyam, that he'd be safe…

But it did matter.

Hadn't he loved her at all? Hadn't she been the world to
him, as he'd been to her, and the moon and the stars, all
rolled into one until the end of time?

She could keep those thoughts at abeyance during the
day. Interviews, networking, phoning old university class-
mates and the people she'd worked with over the years kept
her busy.

It was the nights that were brutal.

She lay awake, remembering Caz with her body, her
heart, her mind. The feel of him, in her arms. The taste of
his skin. The way he'd sat beside her, holding her close as
he talked about his plans for his people.

She dreamed of him, longed for him, ached for him. But
she hadn't cried for him, until now. No tears. None, until
someone who loved her asked a couple of simple questions,
and then the tears she'd kept inside burst free.

Bree led her to the sofa, made soothing noises and patted
her back, kept an arm clamped around her while Megan
wept until there were no tears left. Then she wiped her eyes
with one of the napkins she was still holding and blew her
nose.

"I'm sorry," she said. "I don't know what happened just
now."

Bree took her hand and patted it. "You okay?"

Megan nodded.

"You sure? Good." Bree's voice hardened. "Now tell
me what that son of a bitch did to you."

"It isn't his fault. I—we—I thought I'd fallen in love

with him, and—'' She let out a gusty breath. ''I *did* fall in love with him. And it was a mistake.''

''Because he didn't love you?''

''It's not that simple. He married me, and—''

''He what?''

''He did it because he had to, to save me from... Oh, hell. It's a long story and it doesn't matter, because the marriage wasn't real. It was just for show. You know.''

''No,'' Bree said, staring at Megan, ''I do not know!''

''Don't look like that, Bree! I told you, it wasn't real. Or—or maybe it was, for a little while, until he dissolved it.''

''This guy wasn't just D and D,'' Bree said coldly, ''he's Dark, Dangerous and also Despicable.''

''No. He's not. You don't know anything about him.''

''I know that he talked you into marriage just so he could—''

''That's not the way he tells it.''

Megan and Briana shot to their feet. ''Sean?'' Bree said.

Megan didn't say anything. How could she? It wasn't the sight of her brother standing in the open doorway that left her speechless, although seeing him suddenly appear was a shock.

What froze her into immobility was the man standing behind him.

It was Qasim. Qasim, looking, yes, dark and dangerous. And angry as hell.

''Qasim?'' she whispered.

''Yes,'' he growled, and tried moving past Sean. Sean wouldn't let him.

''You're in my way, O'Connell,'' Caz said coldly.

''Damned right I am,'' Sean said, just as coldly. ''And I will be, until my sister tell me to move.''

''She won't have to. I'll move you myself.''

"Come on." Sean swung around and put his fists up. "I'd love you to try."

"Listen, you thick-skulled baboon—"

"Stop it!" The men looked at Megan. She took a step forward. "Just stop it, both of you. Sean? Qasim? What are you doing here?"

"How come you don't keep your door locked?"

"Don't answer a question with a question, damn it! What are you doing here?"

Sean folded his arms. "This idiot turned up on my doorstep yesterday. I was at my place in New York, and—"

"And," Caz said grimly, "I asked him some questions."

"I don't understand. What questions? What could you possibly want with my brother? How'd you even find him?"

Caz folded his arms, too. "I have ways."

"Bull," Sean said, rolling his eyes. "He has ways? He looked in the phone book, Meg. That's how he found me."

"But—but what for?" She looked at Caz. "Why did you go to see my brother?"

"I told you, I had questions." A muscle knotted in Caz's jaw. "And he couldn't answer them."

Megan shook her head. "I don't know what you're talking about."

"Yeah, you do." Caz glared at her. "I asked him what, exactly, he'd told you the night you phoned him."

"Oh." She felt color flood her face. "Well, I—I—I don't see what business that is of yours."

"You don't, huh? Well, let me spell it out for you, Megan. You said you left me because of what he told you." Caz's mouth thinned. "What he *supposedly* told you."

Megan swallowed dryly. "So?"

"So, why such an elaborate lie? All you had to do was tell me you wanted to end our marriage."

"Marriage?" Sean's voice snapped like a whip. "What

marriage? Listen, Qasim or Caz or whatever the hell your name is, you never said anything about—''

"What's the difference?" Megan said, her eyes fixed on Caz's face. "Our marriage is over. You made sure of that. You divorced me, remember? You said—''

"Is everybody crazy? Bree, what's she talking about? Our Megan was married?''

"Your Megan *is* married," Caz growled.

"I'm not. You dissolved our marriage.''

"Not true.''

"But you said—''

"I lied.''

Megan blinked. "You lied?''

"Damned right.''

"Oh.'' She moistened her lips with the tip of her tongue. "Then—then just saying you divorced me didn't…''

Caz snorted.

"What's so funny?'' Megan said, slapping her hands on her hips and tapping her foot.

"I admit, Suliyam's not a lawyer's paradise but even in my country, divorce isn't that simple. There have to be witnesses to the declaration, papers signed…''

She stared at him. "So we're not…?''

"No. We're not. You're still my wife.''

"Is that why you came here? To tell me we're still married, and that you want a real divorce?''

"You know, *kalila*, for an intelligent woman, you can be awfully stupid.''

"Hey! That's my sister you're—''

"She's my wife,'' Caz said. He looked at Megan and his voice softened. "And you're going to remain my wife, because I won't let you leave me.''

"I already left you,'' Megan said, and told her heart to stop racing. So what if he wanted her back? So what if, by some miracle, he loved her? *She* loved *him,* far too much to let him risk his life, his throne, all he'd worked to achieve for his people. "And why did it take you four weeks to tell me this? Why did you go looking for my brother instead of me?"

"It took me that long because I let my pride get in the way. And I went looking for your brother because I thought he'd talked you into leaving me." Caz smiled a little. "I figured I had two choices, *kalila.* Either I'd change his mind—or I'd beat him into a pulp."

Sean started to speak but Caz ignored him.

"Do you remember that last time we made love?" His eyes darkened. "How we held each other afterward? How you kissed me?"

"Oh, man," Sean said unhappily, "I don't want to listen to this."

"Then don't," Bree said. She put an arm around Megan's shoulders and pressed a quick kiss to her cheek. "Sean and I are leaving."

"No," Sean said, "we are not. I told you, I'm not going anywhere until—"

"I love you, Megan," Caz said, his voice cutting across Sean's. "And you love me."

"I don't. I can't. Hakim said—"

"Hakim lied."

"No. He told me the truth." Tears rose in Megan's eyes and spilled down her cheeks. "They'll take revenge," she whispered. "Alayna's people."

"Nobody wants revenge, sweetheart. The old ways are gone. Hakim just couldn't accept that." Caz's mouth thinned. "When I told Alayna's father there'd be no marriage, he was relieved. He loves his daughter. He would have reneged on the agreement a long time ago, but he was afraid to defy me."

"Oh, Caz. Caz…"

Caz looked at Sean. "You need to get out of my way," he said politely. "Decking a brother-in-law I've only met eight hours ago isn't a good start, but so help me, I'll do it if you try to keep me from my wife a moment longer."

Sean opened his mouth, then shut it. He looked at Megan, whose eyes glittered with tears but whose smile spoke of such joy it made his heart ache.

"You'd better take good care of my sister, pal," he said gruffly, "or you're gonna have to deal with me and two other goons who love her as much as I'm starting to think you do."

Caz grinned and stuck out his hand. "Deal."

"Deal?" Megan said, trying to sound indignant. "You two make like—like a pair of Mr. Machos, then you shake hands and say you've got a deal, and nobody even thinks to ask me what I want?"

Caz moved past Sean and came slowly toward her. "I'm asking you now, wife. What is it you want?"

Megan looked into her husband's eyes. "You," she whispered. "Oh, Caz, I want you. Forever, with all my heart."

Sean jerked his head toward the door. Briana wiped her eyes and nodded. The door swung shut behind them, and Megan flew into her husband's arms.

Mary O'Connell Coyle wanted to make the wedding at the Desert Song Hotel, in Las Vegas.

"Ma," Megan said carefully, "Caz and I thought…"

"If that's what your mother really wants, that's fine, *kalila*," Caz said. He winked at her and pulled some photos from his pocket. "Mary? You want to take a look at these?"

Mary stared at the photos of his palace by the sea. Then she smiled and batted her lashes at her new son-in-law and said one of the best things about being female was that you could change your mind any time you wanted.

It was, of course, a wedding straight out of a fairy tale. The sea, beating softly against the shore. The palace, gleaming white against the perfect blue sky. The gold-tipped spires, the marble walls and silk carpets...

"Isn't it wonderful, Dan?" Mary whispered to her husband, just before he took his stepdaughter up the aisle. "My girls look like princesses."

They did, he agreed.

Briana and Fallon were both Megan's maids of honor. Matron of honor, in Fallon's case.

"Very pregnant matron of honor," her adoring husband said proudly.

Cassie and Marissa, Megan's sisters-in-law, were her bridesmaids. Cullen, Keir, Sean and Stefano were Qasim's groomsmen. After some initial verbal sparring designed to assure themselves he loved Megan enough to suit them, the entire male contingent of the clan had welcomed Caz with open arms.

Everything went smoothly. Even the O'Connell babies stopped squalling and watched Megan as she reached the altar on her stepfather's arm. He kissed her, gave her hand to Qasim, and the look on Qasim's face when he smiled at his bride made Mary weep.

She reached for Dan's hand when he sat down beside her.

"My baby's so beautiful," Mary whispered.

Dan smiled. "She is, indeed."

Another muffled sob. Dan reached into his pocket and took out a big white handkerchief. "Here you go, countess," he said, and his use of his wife's nickname set off another round of tears.

"I love you, Dan Coyle," Mary whispered, "and isn't it a perfect day?"

*   *   *

A perfect day, Sean thought, watching the festivities with a slightly jaded eye.

Well, sure. If you liked that kind of thing, it probably was, but why on earth would a man want to give up his freedom? Women were wonderful creatures, and it was a damned fine thing two of his sisters had found men who'd worship them, damned fine, too, that his brothers had found women they adored.

They were happy, the lot of them. He was happy for them.

But this brand of happiness wasn't for him.

Hell, he thought, running a finger inside the collar of his starched shirt, never him.

Give up the life he loved? The footloose, drop-everything-and-go freedom of it? Forego the thrill of the next toss of the dice, the next turn of the cards for the same four walls every night? A nine-to-five job?

Most of all, definitely most of all, give up the excitement of seeing a beautiful woman, the hot anticipation that came of catching her eye and knowing you'd be bedding her soon? That you'd enjoy her, and she'd enjoy you, until it began to get a little dull?

The chase was everything.

For him, anyway. And it would never change.

Sean turned his attention back to his sister. Megan was looking at Caz as if he were the center of her universe. He was looking at her the same way. Sean felt like a cultural anthropologist at a tribal ceremony, watching the natives go through a ritual he couldn't possibly comprehend.

The judge smiled at the bride and groom. "It is my pleasure," he said, "to pronounce you man and wife."

Everybody applauded, including Sean.

He was applauding his sister's happiness, of course.

And if he was also applauding his own independence, that was nobody's business but his own.

The world's bestselling romance series.

Seduction and Passion Guaranteed!

Your dream ticket to the vacation of a lifetime!

Why not relax and allow Harlequin Presents® to whisk you away
to stunning international locations with our new miniseries...

Where irresistible men and sophisticated women surrender to seduction under the golden sun.

Don't miss this opportunity to experience glamorous lifestyles and exotic settings in:

This Month:
MISTRESS OF CONVENIENCE
by Penny Jordan
on sale August 2004, #2409

Coming Next Month:
IN THE ITALIAN'S BED
by Anne Mather
on sale September 2004, #2416

Don't Miss!
THE MISTRESS WIFE
by Lynne Graham
on sale November 2004, #2428

FOREIGN AFFAIRS... A world full of passion!

**Pick up a Harlequin Presents® novel and you will enter a world
of spine-tingling passion and provocative, tantalizing romance!**

Available wherever Harlequin books are sold.

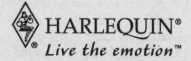

www.eHarlequin.com   HPFAUPD

Harlequin Romance®

A compelling miniseries from Harlequin Romance

From paper marriage...to wedded bliss?

A wedding dilemma:

What should a sexy, successful bachelor do if he's too busy making millions to find a wife, or finds the perfect woman and just has to strike a bridal bargain...?

The perfect proposal:

The solution? For better, for worse, these grooms in a hurry have decided to sign, seal and deliver the ultimate marriage contract...to buy a bride!

Don't miss the latest CONTRACT BRIDES story coming next month by emotional author Barbara McMahon.

Her captivating style and believable characters will leave your romance senses tingling!

September—Marriage in Name Only (HR #3813)

Starting in September,
Harlequin Romance has a fresh new look!

Available wherever Harlequin books are sold.

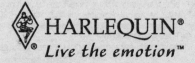

If you enjoyed what you just read,
then we've got an offer you can't resist!

Take 2 bestselling
love stories FREE!
Plus get a FREE surprise gift!

Clip this page and mail it to Harlequin Reader Service®

IN U.S.A.	IN CANADA
3010 Walden Ave.	P.O. Box 609
P.O. Box 1867	Fort Erie, Ontario
Buffalo, N.Y. 14240-1867	L2A 5X3

YES! Please send me 2 free Harlequin Presents® novels and my free surprise gift. After receiving them, if I don't wish to receive anymore, I can return the shipping statement marked cancel. If I don't cancel, I will receive 6 brand-new novels every month, before they're available in stores! In the U.S.A., bill me at the bargain price of $3.80 plus 25¢ shipping & handling per book and applicable sales tax, if any*. In Canada, bill me at the bargain price of $4.47 plus 25¢ shipping & handling per book and applicable taxes**. That's the complete price and a savings of at least 10% off the cover prices—what a great deal! I understand that accepting the 2 free books and gift places me under no obligation ever to buy any books. I can always return a shipment and cancel at any time. Even if I never buy another book from Harlequin, the 2 free books and gift are mine to keep forever.

106 HDN DZ7Y
306 HDN DZ7Z

Name	(PLEASE PRINT)	
Address	Apt.#	
City	State/Prov.	Zip/Postal Code

* Terms and prices subject to change without notice. Sales tax applicable in N.Y.
** Canadian residents will be charged applicable provincial taxes and GST.
   All orders subject to approval. Offer limited to one per household and not valid to current Harlequin Presents® subscribers.
   ® are registered trademarks owned and used by the trademark owner and or its licensee.

PRES04   ©2004 Harlequin Enterprises Limited

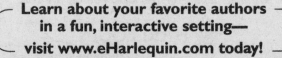

The world's bestselling romance series.

HARLEQUIN®
Presents~

Seduction and Passion Guaranteed!

Legally wed,
Great together in bed,
But he's never said…
"I love you"

They're…

Wedlocked!

The series
where marriages
are made in
haste…and love
comes later….

Don't miss
HIS CONVENIENT MARRIAGE by Sara Craven #2417
on sale September 2004

Coming soon
MISTRESS TO HER HUSBAND by Penny Jordan #2421
on sale October 2004

**Pick up a Harlequin Presents® novel and you will
enter a world of spine-tingling passion and
provocative, tantalizing romance!**

Available wherever Harlequin books are sold.

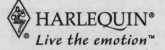

HARLEQUIN®
Live the emotion™